WHISPERS OF TERROR

WHISPS BOOK TWO

JEN HAEGER

SCARSDALE PUBLISHING

For Scott,
I love you more than lollipops.

ACKNOWLEDGMENTS

I don't know how to properly thank everyone who helped me to write this book. From friends and family who understood when I was on "Nanotime" and couldn't attend social events, to my husband who helped brainstorm, beta read, edit, and supported me in countless other ways, to Casey and Sharona and the Scarsdale Publishing team who kept me on my toes and on my deadlines, I couldn't have done this without you.

But I also need to go back a bit. C.P. suggested I do NaNoWriMo. NaNoWriMo got me to write my first novel. Adam Millard and Zoe Ray at Crowded Quarantine Publications published my first series. My fans and fellow authors at PenguinCon and Confusion made me feel like my writing was actually good. Barnes and Noble in Brighton, Michigan, stocks my books on their shelves. And my writer's group keeps me writing. It may seem like a solitary endeavor, but writing is a group effort.

So, all I can say is thank you, and you, and you. You know who you are.

KIRBY IS AN UGLY BUILDING. EVEN WITH THE SUN'S morning rays lighting its impressively tall face, there is nothing pretty about it: no fancy trim to the stone, no statuary, and no pillars. The fact that it houses and treats New York City's criminally insane doesn't help, and the fact that I'm here to visit Rachel Chester really doesn't help. I promised Dr. Fritz I'd see her as part of my therapy, but right now, I'm frozen outside the front doors choking on a bone-dry throat.

It's a totally different sensation from seeing her in Rikers, a totally different fear. This isn't the diabolical murderer trying to invade my head and unravel my psyche. This is the woman I literally drove insane by destroying her WHISP. And I did it knowing what would happen to her. Never mind that her WHISP was trying to murder me and my family at the time, and that she was probably controlling it...probably.

I catch my reflection in the glass, but I can't see my own WHISP today. Not in this bright sunlight. If I just stay in the sun, I can pretend none of this ever happened. I can imagine Chester's still in Rikers atoning for her crimes; I can believe I never jumped into a particle accelerator and developed a WHISP.

Honestly, I could come back another day. But that's a lie. I know if I don't go in now, I will never enter this building again…at least, not willingly.

Every step is like walking through molasses, but I make it to the doors then through them to the security checkpoint. The guard makes me leave my gun. It was stupid to bring it, but it's habit, and if I'm honest, a bit of a security blanket. At reception, a woman with a lovely floral hijab smiles across the counter at me.

"Hello. How can I help you today?"

Deep breath. I take out my badge, also habit. "Hello. My name's Detective Harbinger. I'm here to see Rachel Chester."

The smile evaporates. "I'm sorry, Detective, but Ms. Chester has a very limited number of approved visitors—"

"I'm on the list."

She consults her computer screen. "I see"—then points to a sign-in sheet. "Sign there. I'll call for a security officer to take you."

I hadn't really considered Chester would be in a secure area, but why wouldn't she be? She was a murderer, or her WHISP had been, and who can say what she's capable of without Ray?

"Detective?"

From seemingly out of nowhere, the guard has arrived. Young, but with the dour expression of an eighty-year-old widower, he points to the elevators beyond reception. The chill of the receptionist follows me as we walk away, and I'm not sure if she's put off by my WHISP or if she knows I'm the one who put Chester in here. My escort, name badge Raymond, of all names, says nothing as we enter the elevator. He pushes the 10.

There's no music, so the silence stretches like a piano string, broken only by the ping of the change of floors. I'd love to break the tension, but the walls are closing in and I can't think of a single thing to say other than, "Oh god, oh god, oh god." When the doors finally open, I nearly burst out ahead of Raymond, but manage to stay a step behind him as we head down a white hallway lined with white doors. After we pass an unmanned attendant's station, he stops abruptly and turns.

"Ms. Chester has been in a catatonic state for three months, but don't try to touch her, give her anything, take anything from her, or touch any of her monitors or her IV's. If you think there's a medical problem, there's a red button on the wall near the door to summon a nurse. Otherwise, I will return in fifteen minutes to take you back out. All visits are restricted to fifteen minutes for non-family members. Do you have any questions?"

Locked in a room with Rachel Chester for fifteen minutes. *Is she strapped down? Can I have my gun back?* I shake my head.

He continues down the hall, stops in front of room 1026, and pulls out a card dangling from a lanyard around his neck. My gut tightens as I scan the hallway. It's completely empty. No, that's probably not true. I'm sure there are manned attendant's stations, just recessed so I can't see them. Holding my breath, I hope to catch the chit-chat of nurses between medication distributions but there's only a muffled scream.

"I'll be back in fifteen minutes." Raymond opens a small window at the top of the door and looks through it before swiping his card across a pad next to the door and pulling it open.

Every fiber in my body is telling me to run, to bolt back to the elevator. *You don't want to see this!*

Inside is a cheerful if Spartan room with yellow walls and a hospital bed. Chester sits in a wheelchair facing the single window streaming in sunlight. Next to her, an IV stand and portable monitor unit whir softly. The scent of disinfectant hangs in the air, under it sweat, old saliva, and human waste.

You can do this. I will myself into the room and the door shuts behind me. Terror grips me. *What if Ray is hiding in the sunlight?* But of course, she...it...isn't. I saw to that. *Could she...it...grow back?* I could just stand here the whole fifteen minutes, then answer honestly when Dr. Fritz asked if I'd visited Chester. *Yes, I visited her. I was in her room for fifteen minutes.* But I've come all this way. I have to look her in the eye. Not for him, for me.

Hugging the wall, I edge closer to the figure in the wheelchair. I should probably say something, but I can't break the silence, can't stop listening to the hum of the machines and the soft whisper of Chester's breathing. I can almost see her face now, but a greasy curtain of her hair is in the way. Strands of it billow with every breath. My own breaths are jagged, my heart clogging my throat. Just a few more steps.

Everything goes white as Chester's face comes into view. I'm blinded by the sunlight, my roaring blood blocks out every sound, but eventually I adjust. Here is the monster of my dreams. She looks sad. Drooping, sallow skin houses a shell of a person, blank eyes stare into the light, seeing nothing. My heart slows, but each beat is painful. She wasn't a good person, but she doesn't deserve this. *What have I done?*

I'm sorry.

I can't say the words aloud. *But she could recover, couldn't she?* A few years of healing, of therapy, and she could be a person again. We don't know this is permanent. Any moment, she could jump out of that chair and try to strangle me, just like old times. I know I'm reaching, but it's all I have. I open my mouth: *Snap out of it!* But I can't form words.

A bit of foam has gathered at the corner of her open mouth, and as I stare, one of the bubbles pops. Thoughts break free of my subconscious prison and ruthlessly hurl to the surface of my brain.

That could be you.

CHAPTER 1

Excerpt from Transcript of Session 47:
Dr. Aziz Fritz with Det. S. Harbinger

Fritz: What about your physical relationship with Ben since the change?
Harbinger: That's actually going surprisingly well.
Fritz: Does that bother you?
Harbinger: Why would it bother me?
Fritz: You tell me.

"ADMIT IT, IT'S WEIRD."

Ben blinks, his eyes straying over my shoulder into the shadows beyond then back again. "What? No."

"You're cute when you're lying." I boop his nose with my finger. Ben, my Ben. We're tangled up in sheets, basking in the euphoria of a renewed partnership, a revitalized marriage fueled by a shared near-death experience and reunion of our small family. A year ago, I couldn't have imagined being on a special WHISP Task Force with both my husband and my son. In fact, Ben and I were supposed to have been in a tech-free cabin in Montana by now, sheltered from all things WHISP.

That ship sailed when I climbed into a particle accelerator and got one of my own.

To say I'm still adjusting is an understatement. After a year, I swear there's a pull in the center of my back from the invisible tether between us, I still flinch sometimes when I catch a glimpse of it, and get the sense of someone following me all the time, though the smothering panic attacks are very rare now. Most of the time, I just try to forget it's there. My therapist is constantly reminding me how unhealthy this attitude is, but I've gotten pretty good at ignoring him, too.

Ben sighs. "Okay, okay. Sometimes it's weird, but only..."

"When I'm on top?"

"When I can see her."

My eyebrows twitch. "*Her?*"

"It. I meant, it."

I raise onto an elbow and stare him down. "Please don't tell me you've named my WHISP. That's worse than naming my boobs."

He smirks and reaches out for a gentle grope. "I thought you liked their nicknames."

I bat his hand away and sit up. "Don't change the subject. Did you name it?" I want to be amused that my particle scientist husband who's studying the WHISP phenomenon at its basic level would name mine. It would be akin to an oncologist naming a tumor. But after dealing with Rachel Chester's murderous WHISP, "Ray," I can't find the humor I'm searching for. Irritation itches at the insides of my throat, spoiling the post-coital glow.

"It's not..." He sits up and starts again. "I didn't want to, but one day it just popped into my head and I couldn't get it out."

"Couldn't get what out?"

Ben's skin has paled and taken on a green sheen. His eyes flit away from mine then back again.

"Ben—"

"Liv."

"Liv?" As images of a rock star's actress daughter force their way into my head, the tingles of a smile pull at the corners of my mouth, but they're smothered when I realize it's just a bastardization of my name, like Rachel to Ray.

Ben must see the disgust in my face. "I'm sorry, babe, I know it's…"

"Fucked up?"

"Similar."

I close my eyes and let myself fall back onto my pillow. How long is Rachel fucking Chester going to ruin my life? But really, would any name be better? Jo, Marie, Consuela, Anastasia, Nefertiti…Bob?

Liv.

I have to admit, the name seems to fit. Am I just pissed because I didn't get to name her? No, not her, *it*. Oh, who am I kidding? Liv is totally a chick. My little chicky WHISP. I imagine her under the bed now staring up at the underside of the box springs. When a chill runs through me, I open my eyes.

Ben is staring. "I'm sorry."

I reach up and rub his beard scruff. "I know. It's okay. I mean, it's not okay, okay, but it's okay. It could be worse. Liv is kinda sexy." I'm really trying here.

"Yeah?" Ben kisses the mound between my thumb and forefinger.

Not going to happen now.

The gurgle of Lincoln's shower turning on saves me from having to disappoint Ben on the possibility of a round two. My mind flickers to memories of round one and I wonder again about the thickness of Lincoln's apartment walls. I cringe inwardly.

"He probably won't hear us in the shower." Ben raises an eyebrow.

I point to the clock as a reminder of an earlier, hastily pressed snooze button.

He groans, falling back onto the bed. "Just five more minutes."

I lean over him and kiss him on the nose. "Five minutes more was ten minutes ago."

He opens his eyes and frowns. "I really am sorry. I love you, and I don't want you to think…anything's changed."

"Everything's changed, but I know what you mean."

My cell buzzes on the nightstand and I glance at the clock again. Seven fifty. Almost eight. Almost an appropriate time for someone to call, but not quite. My cop sense comes to life and washes over me like a splash of cold water. I reach for the phone with cold fingers. It's the station. "Harbinger," I say.

"I'd good morning you, Detective, but I don't want to blow smoke up your ass, because we both know that's not true."

Crone isn't officially on the task force, but many of our cases have started as his. "What happened?"

"Hate crime, looks like. Someone hit a WHISP shelter last night."

"Shit. How many?"

"One, for sure."

"Only one?" A single WHISP murder, even at a shelter, wouldn't justify an early morning phone call.

"For sure. There's an unknown number missing from the shelter."

"Missing. Okay." Still not worth this phone call. "What else?"

Crone clears his throat. "There's a guy here from CAW who wants to talk to you about it."

There it is. "An informant?"

"More like a spokesperson. He wants to clear their name in this."

"Kinda early for that, isn't it? If this just happened last

night, how did they even know about it already? Seems a little 'the lady doth protest too much,' doesn't it?"

If Crone gets the reference, he doesn't let on. "Are you coming in, or what?"

"Be there in thirty." I let out a long sigh. Not as bad a call as it could've been this early in the morning.

Ben wraps his arms around me from the side, I note, not behind. "New case?"

I nod. "New case."

———

ON THE WAY TO THE STATION, I ANSWER MY OWN question. Of course, CAW, Citizens Against WHISPs, would know about the shelter. They're probably watching all things WHISP even closer than our little task force does. Still, something smells funny. True, CAW would be the first people we'd want to talk to about a crime like this, yet them heading us off at the pass is strange.

I have visions of CAW's preeminent lawyer, Lila Grant, in her tastefully revealing suit, in the interrogation room, but when I arrive at the station, I can already tell by Crone's sullen demeanor that he hasn't seen anything he's liked this morning.

"What took you so long? Up late at a kegger last night?" Crone chuckles at his own joke.

He's been giving me shit about me and Ben temporarily living with Lincoln, still technically a college student working on his Master's thesis, while we search for a new apartment. I ignore him and point toward interrogation. "So?"

Crone thumbs over his shoulder toward the conference room. "Apparently, we aren't treating Mr. McCaffrey as a suspect quite yet."

"Mr. McCaffrey?"

Crone opens a file. "Rondell James McCaffrey, thirty-three,

previously arrested for petty theft at age fifteen for shoplifting, used to work at a Kwik Lube, now currently employed full-time by CAW as a public relations specialist."

"How does a grease monkey become a public relations specialist?"

"Good question."

I raise my eyebrows. "You didn't ask him anything?"

Crone shrugs. "He says he'll only talk to you. Probably wants your autograph for taking out Ray."

My gut tightens. Rachel Chester's WHISP was trying to kill me and my family, but destroying it broke something in Chester. Having her behind bars because of me was justice, but having her in a psyche ward because of me is something else. "Nah, no one at CAW would want my autograph now that I've got a WHISP." I grab the file from Crone. "Anything you wanna tell me about the crime before I go in there? There's a body, right?"

Crone's grubby fingers snatch up another file on his desk. "Yosef Zimmerman, fifty-eight. There's a Brooklyn address on his driver's license we're following up, but it seems like he was in residence at the WHISP shelter, so he probably had a WHISP. Nothing weird with his murder though, he was just shot."

"Could he have been the target and the other residents just scattered?"

Crone shrugs again. "We're searching for surveillance footage from traffic cams and nearby buildings. We'll probably know more in a few hours." He grins. "You could just get this guy to confess CAW did it and save us all a lot of time."

"Wouldn't that be nice?" I head toward the conference room.

"Go get 'em, tiger."

Behind my back, I give Crone the finger. I wonder if he can see my WHISP doing the same.

CHAPTER 2

Excerpt from Transcript of Session 53:
Dr. Aziz Fritz with Det. S. Harbinger

Fritz: So, you're saying it hasn't affected your work.
Harbinger: Well, no, of course it has. I'm on a WHISP Task
Force now. I just mean, it hasn't affected the quality of my work.
Fritz: But it has limited the scope of your work. Don't you find
that frustrating?
Harbinger: My WHISP didn't limit the scope of my work, I did.
Fritz: Okay. But you didn't answer my question.

RONDELL JAMES MCCAFFREY IS WAY TOO CALM TO BE an informant. Lounging in a chair facing the door, he smiles cordially and rises when I enter. A tall, black man with soft brown eyes and neat, shoulder-length, red-brown hair, his tan shirt, chocolate tweed vest, and khaki pants fairly scream public relations.

"Detective Harbinger, it's an honor to meet you." He rounds the table and proffers his hand.

I take it. His fingers are warm, with the rough callouses of blue-collar work. "Mr. McCaffrey." Releasing his hand, I motion him to sit. "What can I do for you this morning?" I catch him spy Liv over my shoulder and glance away. Not surprising. Even people who don't hate WHISPs are usually put off by them.

His smile fades as he returns to his seat. "I wish we were meeting under better circumstances. Basically, CAW has asked me to come and speak to the WHISP Task Force and personally tell you that CAW had nothing to do with what happened last night."

"And what happened last night?"

"It would be a waste of everyone's time for the police to pursue us as a suspect in this crime."

"What crime?"

The smile returns, but with less mirth. "Detective, I'm sure you know that CAW monitors establishments like the WHISP shelter on Fourth Street. We may be able to help you with your investigation, but in exchange, we'd like the police to not round up the usual suspects in this matter and cause CAW a lot of undeserved bad press."

I snort. "Mr. McCaffrey—"

"Please, call me Rondell."

"Rondell, since this is all off the record, and really just two folks talking with each other, let me tell you something about CAW. I'm sure they come off as a legitimate organization, particularly in the wake of the very rare case of Rachel Chester, but they've done bad things, evil things, and probably still do. Maybe not the people at the weekly meetings, but CAW is a large organization and you shouldn't think you know even a fraction of what goes on in it."

"Detective—"

I hold up my hand to silence him. "And, if you have information about a crime, you have a civic duty to come forward with that information."

He looks down at his hands. "Detective, there may have been a bad…element to CAW in the past, but things in the organization are different now. We're trying to turn over a new leaf, so you can see how important it is for us to not be implicated in something like this without reason."

Unbelievable. People really do believe what they want to believe. I stand. "Rondell, it was very kind of you to come down to the station this morning for a chat, but if you don't have any information for me regarding any crime, I'm afraid I have cases that require my attention. I'll have an officer see you out."

"We have video."

I stare him down. "Of what?"

"Of the abduction of those people."

"Let's pretend just for a moment that it's okay that CAW was surveilling the shelter. You need to give me the footage."

"We had nothing to do with it."

"I'm sure the evidence will prove that out."

He stands. "Why would we give you video of us kidnapping those people?"

I shrug. "You could've faked it."

"Again, why would we do that?"

"To create confusion, and try to get us to look in a different direction when the criminals are right in front of us." I throw his file down on the table.

"I'll give you the footage. Give it to your best techs. It'll stand up. Then, I guess do what you feel is necessary, but remember that we cooperated fully from the very beginning."

I shake my head. "Offering me evidence in exchange for not investigating CAW as a suspect is *not* fully cooperating, and I'll go wherever the evidence takes me."

His serious brown eyes take on a sheen of anger, but the anger fades almost immediately. "Guess that's what makes you a good cop." He reaches into the pocket of his vest and retrieves a memory card. He stares at it a moment before handing it over to me and meeting my eyes. "Please, Detective, we're not the bad guys, not anymore."

I don't blink or smile. "Maybe you should change your name then."

He deliberately looks over my shoulder and focuses on my WHISP, then back at me. "Just because I don't like something doesn't make me a bad person."

"Maybe not, but it doesn't make you a good one, either." I scoop up his file and tap the bottom against the table to straighten its contents.

A small grin. "I guess not. Thank you again for your time."

"Let's hope it wasn't wasted." Holding up the memory card, I turn and walk out of the conference room. I'm really hoping the card is legitimate, for the sake of speeding the investigation. Missing persons cases always have a ticking clock, but if this jackass is wasting my time with CAW political bullshit, I'm going to make sure the task force is up their ass for the next six months. As I close the door, I spy an uni. "Hey, Truman."

A uniformed officer with mousy-brown hair and dull eyes turns from the patrol duty board. "Yeah."

"Can you escort Mr. McCaffrey from the conference room to the exit, please?"

"Okay."

I interpret his tone as '*You got two broken legs, Detective?*' but I've got a possible break in a time sensitive case burning a hole in my hand. Never mind that I'm not actually on the case yet. I expect that call from the Chief, now acting commander of the WHISP Task Force, any minute now. There's still a little bureaucracy around us, about which cases are officially under our jurisdiction, and occasionally there's some unofficial bitching and moaning about handing cases over to us, but this case is pretty much what the task force was set up for.

Crone looks up from his desk and sees my face. "What've you got?"

Barely slowing as I pass his desk, I pick up the kidnapping case file. "Who's in tech this morning?"

He jumps up. "Baker? I don't know. Why?"

I wave the memory card in front of his face. "We may have footage of the crime."

Too jumpy to take the elevator, I hit the staircase and ascend.

Crone, an extra forty pounds dragging him down, lags behind. "This isn't your case, you know."

I pass the second floor on my way to the third and call over the railing, "Not yet!"

———

BY THE TIME CRONE JOINS BEAULIEU AND ME IN THE tech and cybercrimes department, she's already determined that the footage on the card hasn't been messed with in any obvious way. The angle is of the front of the building, but is a better shot of the sidewalk and door than of the street. We're fast forwarding to the night in question when Crone catches his breath.

"Well?"

Beaulieu answers without taking her eyes off the screen, "So far, I haven't detected anything unusual about the footage, the time stamp is tracking and the new software says there hasn't been any editing or deletions."

"We're just getting to last night," I say.

Beaulieu slows the footage down to real time. "When did it happen?"

I turn to Crone, but he shrugs. "No idea. Body was found around five when a janitorial service showed up to clean the bathrooms or something. Coroner hasn't pinned down a TOD yet. A window was broken in the room the body was in."

No need for him to explain further. It's February in New York City. Cold bodies abound, making easy body temp TODs near impossible. "Shit."

"It's fine. I'll skip ahead to 5 a.m. then backtrack."

After a little fine finagling, we spot the cleaning service arriving at 5:17 a.m. and begin rolling back the video. Each rewound minute is like an hour of my life I'll never get back as we all stare at the screen. McCaffrey said he caught a kidnapping on this memory stick, but even backed up to 3 a.m., I'm seeing nothing unusual. I rub my blurring eyes. "Is there a back door to this place?"

Crone blinks at me. "Yeah, but it was still locked and would've triggered an alarm."

I return my gaze to the screen. "If this card has nothing useful on it, I'm gonna be seriously pissed."

"What did that CAW asshole say was on it?"

"Oh nothing, just proof that someone else was responsible."

"There!"

Beaulieu has paused the video and is pointing to the screen where a white van has just backed into frame.

"Can't see the damn license plate," Crone mutters.

"Why is it always a white van?"

Beaulieu begins the slow rewind again, but even slower. The van, with all windows whited out except the windshield, driver's, and passenger's, backs into a spot in front of the WHISP shelter. Six individuals in white hazmat suits get out carrying covered stretchers with sheets hanging down and dragging along the ground. Sluggishly, they back into the shelter.

"What the fuck?"

Crone takes the words right out of my mouth. I'm not sure what I was expecting, but it wasn't this. This isn't some snatch and grab WHISP terrorism bullshit. If I didn't know better, and the van was marked, I'd guess this was the CDC responding to some kind of outbreak. Should I be calling the CDC? Would they even tell the local authorities if there was a contained case of Ebola or something? Then I remember the murder victim.

The CDC wouldn't have shot him, and if they had, they probably would've taken his body either to hide the fact that they'd shot someone or because he'd also been exposed to whatever the people on the stretchers had been exposed to. Bioterrorists are another possibility, but they would've left all the bodies, wouldn't they?

"Um…do you think we should notify the coroner about the suits?" I ask. "Could've been a test from a bioterrorist group maybe?"

Crone's face has gone pale and slack. "I was at that crime scene for about an hour."

I resist the urge to pull away from him. "How do you feel?"

"I felt fine until now. Now, maybe dizzy, light-headed?"

Beaulieu is nonplussed. "Probably just from watching this video backwards. Used to make me dizzy, too. Let's skip ahead now and play it forward in real time, then we can slow it down again."

Crone swallows hard and fidgets in his seat. As Beaulieu tries to pinpoint the van's arrival, I've already got my cell out and am calling Claire Buckingham at the Office of the Chief Medical Examiner. No answer. Not unusual if she's elbow-deep in a corpse. I text in lieu of a message.

Harbinger: Maybe something up with Zimmerman body. Something contagious or weaponized. Call me.

I don't want to start a panic for no reason. It's possible the suits are for disguise and to minimize evidence left behind, but still, I feel like I have to say something to somebody just in case.

"McCaffrey coulda told us there was something scary like this on the footage."

"What do you expect? Those CAW assholes didn't even call the police when it happened. Coulda fucking warned us."

"Maybe they weren't monitoring this video feed all night.

Maybe they only saw what happened in the morning when they were reviewing the video."

Crone's face goes from pale to sunburned. "And maybe they're behind this thing and didn't hand over the video until they'd double-checked to make sure we couldn't tell it was them."

"That's possible." I'm pissed Crone thinks I'm defending CAW when I'm just thinking out loud, but I'm even more pissed at McCaffrey. How the Hell could he be so nonchalant about this? How could he waste my time babbling about CAW's fucking public image when there were biohazard suits and stretchers? And why had he said kidnapping? Anyone who'd seen the tape would've assumed people on those stretchers were dead. Either he hadn't seen the tape or CAW was involved and he *knew* they weren't dead...yet. Regardless, I'd be talking to him again soon, and not in the conference room.

With the footage now cued up from the first appearance of the van at 2:17 a.m., Beaulieu faces us. "Ready?"

I nod and the van pulls into the spot in front of the shelter, but there's nothing notable about it and I can't see the license plate or anyone inside through the tinted windows. For a full minute, nothing happens. Then six figures in white suits surge out from the side of the van and head into the shelter. Two look like they're carrying shotguns and the other four are carrying large duffle bags that might contain the stretchers collapsed down. I want to get a closer look at the weapons, but I also want to see how the whole thing plays out first. After the six figures disappear inside, there's nothing to see for several minutes.

"Wasn't there any security?"

Crone's cheeks are still flushed, but he seems to be recovering from his mild shock. "There was a lock on the inner door, but it wasn't a very good one. Looks like they smashed right through it."

"And no surveillance cameras on the inside?"

"Nope. Shelter wouldn't work if people thought Big Brother was watching."

"Right." My phone buzzes, but it's not Claire, it's the Chief. "Harbinger."

"We've got a new case."

"WHISP shelter on Fourth Street. I know. I'm on it. We're watching video now."

There's a brief hiccup of silence on the Chief's end. "From traffic cameras?"

"Surveillance footage from CAW. I'll tell you later. For right now, Chief, this may be something bad."

"Bad how?"

"Bioterrorism? I don't know. There are people in hazmat suits, stretchers, an unmarked white van..."

"I thought it was a homicide and a kidnapping."

"Maybe not."

CHAPTER 3

Excerpt from Transcript of Session 41:
Dr. Aziz Fritz with Det. S. Harbinger

Fritz: Let's talk about physical symptoms for a moment.
Harbinger: I don't have any.
Fritz: Most WHISPers report fatigue, light-headedness, some-times an itching or tingling in the center of their back. You haven't experienced anything like that?
Harbinger: I don't think so, but the burns on my back are still healing, so it's hard to say.

ABOUT AN HOUR LATER, I'M CROSS-EYED FROM examining the video and trying to glean any more information from it. As a precaution, the Chief locked down the shelter in a biohazard protocol and Claire did the same with the body and called in the city health department. I look up to ask Crone if he's seen anything new and find he isn't there. I rub my eyes and Beaulieu stops the playback again. After dissecting the footage of the crime, we've moved on to viewing the day before to see if we can find any answers.

"When did Crone leave?"

"About a half-hour ago. He got a text and took off."

Now that she's said it, I vaguely remember him getting a text. "Right." A wave of nausea rolls over me as I try to focus on the screen again. "I should follow up with him. You'll call me if you find anything I need to see?"

"Sure."

I rise and the nausea follows. Trying not to run, I head out and find the nearest bathroom, making it to the sink just as the bile rises up the back of my throat. Open-mouthed breathing, I splash cold water on my face and manage not to puke. Still feeling a bit queasy, I head down to find Crone. I could call or text him, but I feel like I need to walk. What I really want to do is get an arrest warrant for Rondell McCaffrey for withholding evidence, but I already know it wouldn't hold up in court. He could easily claim that CAW did hand over the recording as soon as they knew there was evidence of a crime and since my conversation with McCaffrey trying to use the video to garner favor wasn't recorded, it'd be his word against mine. Besides, as a public relations monkey, he may really not have seen the video. Still, someone told him it was a kidnapping, so CAW had to know more than they were saying. Even though they had helped get me some needed WHISP information in the past, I hated being dicked around by them. Also, once word got around the station that I'd been personally requested by a CAW representative and gotten the video from them, rumors would start flying.

Focus Harbinger. Forget about CAW for right now. Focus on finding those missing people.

I spot Crone at his desk and make a beeline for him. "What have you got?"

"Well, we finally talked to some shelter employees and got an idea of how many people are missing."

"How many?"

"Four. Three women and a man. We're waiting on a subpoena to get the names. The shelter is huge on privacy."

I flop down at the empty desk across from Crone. Jaeger won't mind. "Four? But there were only three stretchers."

"Maybe they doubled up on one."

"Or maybe one got away and went into hiding. I'll tell Beaulieu to double check for anyone leaving between the time the janitor showed up and when the first cop got there." I shoot off a quick text to her. "Where are we on the traffic cam footage?"

"Well, that's not good news. The city's whole traffic cam system is being updated and half of them are out right now."

"You're kidding me."

Crone leans back in his chair. "Wish I was. Right now, we're pulling any active cam footage in a two-mile radius, but since we don't have a license plate, we're just looking for white vans driving by within thirty minutes of the crime. If we find anything, we'll move the radius to the next ring of active cameras, but if we're able to catch the van at all, it'll take a while to track it this way and once it's out of the city—"

"We're out of luck." I tap a fingernail against my teeth. "What about toll booths? We could estimate how long it would take the van to reach a booth and then look at video from..." Crones face is grim. "Don't tell me, they're updating the cameras at the toll booths, too."

"Yep."

"Sonofabitch! That's fucking lucky for the abductors."

Crone raises an eyebrow. "You keep saying kidnappers and abductors, but I thought you thought this was some kinda bioterrorist attack and they took the bodies to study them or something."

"One, I want to believe those people are still alive and two, CAW said they were kidnapped."

"Why would they say that based on that video surveillance?"

"I don't—" My phone buzzes.

Beaulieu: something you should see.

"Beaulieu has something, you coming?"

"Nah. Gonna dig into this shelter some more. See if they've received any specific threats recently." He fiddles with a pen on his desk. "This'll be your little task force's first big case since..."

Chester. Neither of us have to say it. The silence is cop-speak for, *Are you ready for this?*

"Yeah. We haven't seen anything like this since the beginning." *It's been a year. I'm ready.*

He picks up his desk phone. "Well, better not fuck it up, then."

"Thanks."

I head back up the two flights to tech. Beaulieu's red eyes are screaming for coffee. After she shows me what she's got, I'll get her some. "What've you got for me?"

On the screen in front of her, she's zoomed in on the weapons two of the suited figures carry and she points to them. "There."

They're not shotguns like I first thought, wrong profile. Instead they almost look like, "Tranquilizer guns?"

She nods. "That's my best guess."

Pulling at my lip, I nod. It's probably why CAW knew it was a kidnapping. Something else strikes me. "Fast forward to when they come out again."

Beaulieu obliges.

The sheets hanging down from the stretchers. "To hide the WHISPs."

"What?"

I point at the white cloth trailing along the cement. "It seemed really weird to me at first to have these sheets. I mean, why have them hanging down like that where they could snag on something or trip you up? But if there are sedated people with WHISPs on those stretchers then—"

"Then it makes sense to have them hanging down to obscure the WHISPs."

Taking the seat next to her, I frown. "That's a lot of fore-thought."

"Well, the whole thing does seem well-planned."

"Maybe a little too well-planned. Did you know that half the traffic cameras in the city are out right now for a system update?"

She nods. "I did, but only because tech got a memo about it a few weeks ago. Said we might need to get more creative to track vehicles. I think they put Raj on a project to look into private surveillance cameras that may have angles of the nearby streets."

"Too bad the shelter was in a rundown part of town."

"Van had to go somewhere, right? And with that many people and stretchers, it would've made it hard to switch vehicles."

A sigh escapes. I hadn't considered the possibility of them switching vehicles until now. Stupid. "Maybe." I want to be optimistic, but really, with how organized the whole thing seems, there's every possibility they switched vehicles. Where would you go from your typical white crime van? A black van? A moving truck? "Regardless, we should probably have unies canvas a three-block radius for a ditched white van." Another sigh. "Any sign of our missing shelter victim?"

Shaking her head, Beaulieu stretches. "If they got away, they didn't do it through the front door."

"Okay, thanks."

"Sure." She rewinds the video to the beginning, the morning of the attack, blinks several times and then starts it in real time. "You might want to ask your buddies at CAW if they'll hand over the previous week's surveillance. Might catch someone casing the shelter or the van practicing the route."

And so it begins. "Those people are not my buddies." I glance over my shoulder at Liv glancing over her shoulder. *At least not now.* "But I'll ask." I wish I could subpoena it, and rattle their cage, but they could be dicks and erase the footage. Hell, since this footage didn't go through any official channels, they could claim it didn't even come from them. *Shit.* I walked right into that. I'm losing my touch. I leave without getting Beaulieu coffee. Petty, I know, but she started it. I want to follow up with Raj and his alternate surveillance project, but I've got to hand that over to Crone. I've got other fish to fry.

After filling Crone in on the tranquilizer guns and Raj's project, I'm at my official desk in the WHISP Task Force office in the basement dialing Rondell McCaffrey's work number at CAW. Someone picks up on the fourth ring.

"Rondell McCaffrey."

Hey asshole. "Mr. McCaffrey, this is Detective Harbinger, we met this morning."

"Of course, Detective. And please call me Rondell. What can I do for you?"

"I need more of CAWs footage of the shelter"—a thought pops into my head—"and footage of any other WHISP shelters CAW's monitoring."

A pause. "I take it our footage was useful to you?"

A plethora of responses run through my head, but I settle on one without profanity. "Would've been more useful had you guys called 9-1-1 right away and reported the crime."

"You make it sound like we had someone there holding the camera."

"You didn't?"

A longer pause. "Let me talk to some people and see what I can get for you. Is there anything in particular you're looking for?"

"Not that I'm at liberty to say. And I'd really appreciate a timely response. I'd hate to have to subpoena the footage from CAW. Might lead to bad press." I know I shouldn't push, but I'm so ticked off I can't help it.

"You understand that, officially, we have no footage of anything, right?"

"And you understand that people's lives are at stake, right? If CAW truly is turning over a new leaf, they should care about stuff like that."

His voice is stiff. "I'll let you know as soon as I have something, Detective."

"I'll thank you when you do."

When McCaffrey hangs up, my shoulders are squeezing my neck. Lowering them, I tilt my head back and rock it from one shoulder to the other. Really, this whole thing stinks of something CAW would do. Lila Grant pretty much admitted to me they did experiments on people with WHISPs, and where better to find guinea pigs than a WHISP shelter? The only problem with my theory is that since the task force began, it's had eyes on CAW. It would've been crazy not to. We'd have known if something big like this was going down either from an increase in activity at their buildings or in their accounts, and they've been quiet for months. Still, it's possible we don't know all that's going on. Like I'd told McCaffrey, CAW is a big organization and there are probably roots to it we don't know about.

What I really want to do is see the crime scene for myself, but it's still being cleared for biohazards. I glance at my watch: 4:00 p.m. Lunchtime has come and gone with me none the wiser. No wonder I have a splitting headache in spite of coffee. The twinge of betrayal I always feel on behalf of the victims when I pause a case courses through me, but I have to eat or I'll be useless if we catch a break in the case later. Since I rushed out this morning with only half a bagel in my mouth, my options are junk food out of the dispenser, ordering something to the station, or heading out in the cold to the polish sausage vendor on the corner. At the mere thought of sausage with mustard and sauerkraut, my stomach flips and my mind is made up.

I grab my coat, head upstairs, and pause at Crone's desk. "Going to the sausage stand. Wanna come?"

He looks up then pointedly at his watch then back at me. "Early dinner?"

"Late lunch. Anything pop with your shelter research?"

"Nah. They've only been operating six months. Had the usual threats, but nothing stood out. None of the employees noticed anything strange or particularly upsetting."

"Anything with the traffic cams yet?"

"I told them to let you know as soon as they found anything." Crone gives me a wry smile. "You remember, I'm not on the case anymore, this is all task force now."

I had actually forgotten. This being the first big case since Chester, and having worked that case with Crone, it just felt like I should be working with him again. "I know. Why aren't you on the task force again?"

"Forget that mess. I want nothing to do with all that weirdness and politics."

I don't blame him. My stomach growls and Crone raises an eyebrow.

"Sure you don't want anything?" I ask.

"Nah, I don't have any hot cases right now. I'm going home for dinner tonight."

After giving him the finger for the second time today, I struggle into my coat, turn, and head for the door.

CHAPTER 4

Excerpt from Transcript of Session 34:
Dr. Aziz Fritz with Det. S. Harbinger

Fritz: Is it the same nightmare? The one with your parents?
Harbinger: Yes, but it's different now. It changes.
Fritz: In what way?
*Harbinger: Sometimes Chester is in it, and sometimes it's Ben
and Lincoln being killed instead of my parents.*
Fritz: Do the nightmares ever feature your WHISP?
*Harbinger: I don't really think this is helping. Can we talk about
something else?*

THE CHILL WIND FROM THIS MORNING HAS
sharpened and bites right through my wool coat as I fight its
bluster to the corner, pulling out a hat and gloves as I go. No
matter what the weather, there are always people on the street
in the city, but today is cold enough to keep many indoors. This
is the part of winter I hate. The post-Christmas, bitter cold but
without the snow to make things pretty. The sausage vendor
seems underdressed with just a vest to compliment his hat and

scarf, but I guess his cart keeps him warm. I order my sausage, dig out my wallet from my coat pocket, and am finally heading back when another underdressed individual catches my eye.

A woman in a robe and stocking feet stumbles across the street toward the precinct. Her wild black hair flies around her head with each gust of wind, giving her WHISP a medusa-like appearance, and her jagged gait has all the traits of a rabbit with a wolf snapping at its heels. I know those too-round eyes and gaunt face. Someone's after her, pimp or ex-husband, I have no way of knowing. Not wanting to spook her, I double my pace and reach the steps just as she makes it to the top. I stop and stare up and down the street to make sure no one is following her, stash my sausage in my coat pocket, then launch up the steps to make sure I intercept her before she reaches the desk. As I suspected, she's stopped just inside the door and looks ready to bolt.

"Hey there. Are you okay? Can I get you a coffee to warm up?"

She spins and backs away so fast that she trips over her own feet and goes down hard on the linoleum. The front of her robe has come open and underneath, her baby blue pajamas with little white clouds are smeared with blood.

"Jung! Call an ambulance!"

The officer manning the front desk looks over at me and the woman on the floor and then grabs the phone.

The woman is shaking her head and trying to get to her feet. "No. No doctors! No!"

I grip her arm as gently as I can without letting her twist away. "But you're bleeding. Please. Let us help you."

Confusion clouds her face, but then she seems to notice the blood on her pajama shirt. "It's not mine." The confusion is replaced by desperation as she stares up at me. "It's not mine! Please, no doctors! Please!"

The proper thing would be to get her to a hospital anyway. Sometimes people in shock don't realize they've been injured, but the woman's pleas stab right in my heart. Now there's a crowd around us and I can tell she's feeling cornered. If I'm going to get anything out of her that I can use to help her, I need to deescalate this fast.

"Listen. Here, I'm Detective Harbinger. Me and..." I scan the mob for another friendly female face and spot a perky uniformed officer with red hair and dimples. Perfect. I point to her. "Officer..." I twirl my hand at the female cop.

She finally gets it. "Oh. Um, O'Hea." She kneels down on the other side of the terrified woman. "Officer O'Hea. Jennie."

"Officer O'Hea and I are going to take you into the conference room and we're just going to sit down a minute. If you're really all right then we'll only have the paramedics take a quick look to make sure. No doctors, just the paramedics, okay?"

I'm not sure the bloody woman really hears me or understands, but she nods, and O'Hea and I get her up between us. Half-leading and half-carrying her, we finally get her into a chair in the conference room.

"O'Hea, can you get her a glass of water?"

The officer leaps into action and is out the door. I turn my attention back to the bloody woman. "My name's Sylvia."

Barely a whisper. "Isabel."

"Isabel. Are you sure nothing hurts?"

She nods, but tears well and fall.

"Do you want to tell me what happened?"

She nods, but O'Hea returns with the water. I'm annoyed by her timing.

"Can you go wait for the paramedics and direct them back here?"

Handing me the water, O'Hea nods and disappears again. I proffer the Styrofoam cup to Isabel. She takes it with a trembling hand. As she sips, I notice dark circles under tan eyes with long Latino lashes. She could be a homeless woman or a junkie, but I'm not catching the distinct scent of either. Also, her pale peach, terry cloth robe and her pajamas are relatively clean and lack holes or tears. Her socks are a little dirty, but not living-on-the-street-without-shoes dirty. Maybe she came from a shelter. A shelter...

Couldn't be.

"Isabel?"

She looks up from the cup of water.

"Did you come from the WHISP shelter? The one on Fourth Street?"

The whites of her eyes are crisscrossed with red. She nods.

"Is that blood Yosef's?"

She nods again.

"Did you see what happened? To Yosef, to the others?"

Paramedics burst through the door and Isabel is on her feet and knocking over chairs to get away from them. *Shit!* I try to calm her down again. Thank God they're blocking the only door.

"Shhhh, shhhh, it's okay, Isabel. They just need to make sure you're all right. I won't let them take you anywhere, I promise."

One of the paramedics shoots me a dirty look, but I couldn't care less. If this is our only eyewitness to the crime last night, I'm not letting her out of my sight.

SOMETIME DURING THE PARAMEDIC'S EXAMINATION of Isabel, my stomach reminds me that I never ate my Polish sausage. I withdraw it from my coat pocket. Suddenly dizzy with hunger, I cram roughly half of it into my mouth as I notice

O'Hea hovering in the corner. As I choke down my mouthful of bread, meat, and sauerkraut, I motion her over. Resisting the urge to send her to the machines for a Coke, I instead smile and wipe mustard off my mouth with a ragged napkin.

"Thanks for your help, O'Hea, but you don't have to stay."

"Oh, it's okay, Detective, I was going off shift anyway." Her eyes flick to Isabel and back. "Did she say what happened to her?"

I want to finish my sadly belated lunch, but after ordering O'Hea around like a dog earlier, I feel a little guilty. "You hear about the 10-71, 10-57 at the WHISP shelter last night?"

She nods like she's six and I just asked her if she wanted ice cream.

"She's part of that."

"Everyone's heard about it. Um..." She glances back at Isabel. "Shouldn't she be quarantined or something? I heard it was some kind of outbreak."

Oops. Maybe. Damn. "Why do you think we brought her in here out of that crowded lobby?" I pretend that my phone just buzzed and I send off a rapid text to the Chief. I need to let him know about the potential witness anyway. Man, am I off my game. I blame a serious lack of blood sugar and almost shoot off another text to Crone demanding a Coke before I realize he's probably gone home already. Then I check my e-mail for any updates on the case. Then I text Crone anyway, just to bug him. O'Hea's waiting patiently for me to finish texting. Now I'm feeling extra guilty since I may have exposed her to something. Checking her for any traces of blood from Isabel's shirt, I motion her to sit. "Truth is, we don't really know what happened and this lady is a potential witness."

"Wow. An eyewitness. That's huge."

I nod. "Could be." The hunger ache in my head is spreading. Guilt or no, I take another bite of sausage, though somewhat smaller than the last. We sit in silence for about fifteen minutes while I methodically finish off lunch, and then another ten while I watch the paramedics work on Isabel.

O'Hea finally clears her throat. "Is it true—"

"Detective." One of the paramedics stands and motions me over. I smile grimly at O'Hea and join him a few feet from where the other paramedic has Isabel on a gurney.

"So, how is she?"

"She's still pretty much in shock, but we can't find any injuries. The blood isn't hers, unless she had a massive bloody nose earlier. We're administering some fluids for slight dehydration and we wrapped her feet up. She's lucky she didn't get frostbite. What happened to her again?"

"We're not entirely sure, but we think she's a potential witness to crime from last night."

"All right, but I'd still recommend she be taken to the hospital for x-rays to rule out any internal injuries and blood-work to rule out—"

The door flies open and what seems like an army clad in hazmat suits marches in. Isabel starts screaming and I've got my gun in my hand before I recognize the Chief in one of the suits.

"A little help here!" The paramedic beside Isabel is trying to keep her on the gurney as she thrashes, and the one I've been talking to rushes to his aid. I assume they sedate her because soon the screaming stops.

"Stand down, Harbinger."

My gun is still in my outstretched hand. I lower it and replace it in my holster. "I take it they haven't cleared the shelter yet."

The Chief stops a few feet from me. Behind him, a wall of plastic sheeting is being erected in front of the door. "This is just a precaution."

"For how long?"

"Maybe twelve hours."

I look back at O'Hea, still sitting at the conference table, and sigh. "Then I'm gonna need a few things from you, Chief."

"Oh yeah? Like what?"

I face him again. "A two-liter of Coke and an extra-large pizza, for starters."

CHAPTER 5

Excerpt from Transcript of Session 31:
Dr. Aziz Fritz with Det. S. Harbinger

Fritz: How do you think Lincoln is adjusting to your WHISP?
Harbinger: Lincoln? I'm sure he's fine, I mean, glad. He's not
alone anymore. We're closer now. Getting along better.
Fritz: Have you asked him how he feels about it?
Harbinger: I don't have to.

EVEN HAVING NEVER BEEN QUARANTINED BEFORE, I could tell it was going to suck, and the worst part was that I couldn't interview Isabel because they'd had to sedate her. Then there was the freezing cold decontamination shower, groovy hospital scrubs they gave me to wear, and the extensive physical examination complete with blood draw and urinalysis by the quarantine response team. At least, the Chief made good on the pizza and Coke and the people in the hazmat suits thought to set up a portable bathroom in one corner. The paramedics were good and pissed, especially when they weren't allowed to continue care on Isabel. They took their pizza at the far end of the conference table while O'Hea and I stuffed ourselves on our end.

After my belly is finally full and my mouth empty, I say to O'Hea, "I'm sorry. I really didn't know who she was when she came in. I had no idea she was from the shelter. I thought she was just another junkie or domestic abuse case."

O'Hea smiles. "Sure, sure, I know."

I'd already called Ben and told him what happened. He took the news of my quarantine fairly well after I explained what we saw on the video. He wanted to suit up and come see me, but I told him not to. No one else's family would've been allowed to come in, so it would've been a dick move. Technically, the lab he ran, and Lincoln worked at, was part of the WHISP Task Force, but we really didn't interact on a daily basis. They did the particle research and we worked the cases until questions arose about WHISP particle properties. Ben had actually had to prepare an affidavit for court that said, although it was rarely possible for WHISP particles to move objects, it wasn't possible for them to transport items such as jewelry or cash through solid walls. Insurance claim denied.

I scan O'Hea's fingers for a ring. Nada. "Hope you didn't have big plans for tonight."

"Oh. No. Probably just watching T.V. with my cats."

I nod. "I'm not sure I've seen you around the precinct before. How long have you been here?"

Her cheeks go crimson. "Honestly? Um, today was my first shift as an officer."

"Oh. Well. Hell of a first day. So, how did it go before I got you quarantined?"

"Fine. We got a B and E call and one domestic. Nothing too exciting." Her cheeks go a shade darker. "Do you remember your first day?"

Like it was yesterday. Watched a kid involved in a gang fight bleed out. "Pretty much the same. Nothing too exciting." No sense in crushing her soul just yet. But I also don't like where this conversation is going, old cop regaling the rookie with all their back-in-my-day stories. I glance down at the paramedics. "I'm gonna see if they're ready to speak to me yet. See if Isabel said anything else before they sedated her and maybe ask when that sedative might wear off."

"Right, sure." O'Hea pulls out her newly sterilized phone in an it's-fine-you-don't-have-to-babysit-me way.

I get up and make my way down the table to cold stares.

"Listen, I'm really sorry. I didn't know who she was when I called you."

"Could've at least given us a heads up they were coming." The one I'd spoken to before, Walsh, by his nametag, hitches a thumb toward the few remaining white suits.

"I wasn't sure they were. I thought they might've cleared the other scene."

"The lady seemed healthy. Just what is it we might've been exposed to?" asks the other paramedic, Fuller, if I remember correctly.

It hadn't occurred to me that the containment team hadn't told them anything. So much for comradery amongst health professionals. No wonder they're so grumpy. "There was a kidnapping last night—"

"What does a kidnapping have to do with—"

I raise a hand and Fuller shuts up. "And the perps were wearing hazmat suits."

Walsh raises an eyebrow. "Where the hell was this kidnapping? A research lab? If it was at NYU, it was probably some PETA bullshit stunt."

I weigh how much I should tell them about an active case. They aren't cops like O'Hea. They might not know when to keep their mouths shut, especially if the press gets wind they were involved in a quarantine. "Not the university and not somewhere they were working with diseases. Probably, they wore suits to prevent being identified and to prevent leaving behind evidence. This is just a precaution."

Fuller snorts. "Precaution. That's what they said."

"Did Isabel say anything while you were checking her out? Anything about the crime, what she saw?"

The paramedics eye each other. Walsh nods. "She didn't say much, just that her friend was dead. That they tried to take him and he fought back and they shot him. I thought you said this was a kidnapping."

Huh. Why shoot someone you wanted to kidnap with a real gun when you could've shot him with a tranquilizer dart? "One fatality." So far…that we know. Damn, I feel useless in here. Wish I'd asked the Chief who was going to be working the traffic cam and private surveillance video overnight. I glance over at Isabel's gurney. They've strapped her down so it's a little hard to tell if she's awake, but she isn't struggling and the suits are watching her monitors, not her. "How long do you think she'll be out?"

Walsh shrugs. "Hard to say with the state she was in. Maybe another couple hours."

Hours. The vacant time trapped in this room yawns out in front of me. After my massive pizza lunch/dinner, the tendrils of sleepiness are wending their way through my body, but even if I were home snug in my own bed instead of in one of the provided cots, I know I wouldn't be able to sleep. Maybe if I ask nicely, the Chief will let me have a laptop.

"Thanks, guys."

The paramedics barely respond as I pull out my phone and walk back toward O'Hea, but I'm done apologizing for all of this. It's not my fault the kidnappers wore hazmat suits. I finish tapping out my request to the Chief and plop down again next to O'Hea. His reply comes too quickly.

Chief: We're on it. Get some rest.

Crap. Now what?

O'Hea looks up from her phone. "Anything useful?"

"Not really. She didn't say much before they sedated her and she'll be out a few hours yet."

"That sucks." She pushes around a pizza crumb on the table. "I wonder how she got away."

Good question. I push back in my seat and crack my neck. "Well, it's possible the kidnappers could've left her behind for some reason, but I don't think she'd have run from the shelter if that was the case. I suppose they could've somehow missed her, then she woke up, found her friend dead, and bolted. Or maybe she only pretended to be tranqed, fought them off somehow, and got away. But most likely she hid and escaped sometime after the attack."

"Tranqed?"

"Oh, yeah. The perps had what looked like tranquilizer guns."

O'Hea's face twists. "Treating them like animals."

I hadn't thought about it like that, but she's right. A prickling chill runs down my spine and I picture the foggy cloud of my WHISP shivering.

O'Hea's eyes snap up to mine. "Oh my God. I'm sorry, Detective. I didn't mean..."

Shaking my head, I smile. "No offense taken." My mind rolls over to my conversation with Lila Grant from CAW. She didn't have a ton of respect for human life when it came to people with WHISPs, but I'm not sure I see her as treating them like cattle, either.

My phone buzzes. Ben's calling. I rise and wander into as private an area as possible. "Hey you."

"Miss you. How's your quarantine going?"

I glance around from O'Hea fiddling with her phone again to the surly paramedics still nibbling on slices of pizza, to the two remaining white suits typing on plastic-coated computers.

"Pretty boring, actually. No one's coughing or bleeding from their eyes yet."

"That's not funny."

"Sorry. How're you? How's Lincoln? You guys order in or did Lincoln make something?"

Ben scoffs with false offense. "Why do you assume I didn't cook?"

"Did you?"

"No."

I smile into the phone. "Uh-huh."

"He made waffles."

"Breakfast for dinner. I like it. So, how's research going? Any luck with inducing WHISPs in animals yet?" Without animal homologs, and serious political issues hampering volunteer WHISP studies, the WHISP research had been slow going thus far.

"Nope. But Lincoln thinks there's still hope. We know the exposure has to be long-term, and most of the experiments are only a year old."

Stifling a yawn, I cradle the phone and stretch out my arms. A hand on my shoulder sends the phone clattering to the floor. Thankfully, my phone cover keeps it from becoming a dead brick with a cracked screen.

"Sylvy! Sylvy! What was that?"

I spin around and find myself face to face with one of the white suits. A black woman with curly hair pulled back into a bun inside the mask of her suit.

"Detective, it's time for another blood draw."

Swallowing down my rabbiting heart, I scoop up the phone. "Sorry, sorry. I dropped my cell. I have to let you go. I'm getting another super-fun blood draw. I love you."

"Love you, too. Let me know when you're sprung."

"Will do." I end the call and pocket the phone then raise my eyebrows at the woman.

"Sorry I startled you." She motions me over to one of the conference chairs they've coated in plastic.

"Wouldn't a bioweapon have gone off by now?" I roll up my sleeve.

The woman doesn't pause in her deft handling of needles and test tubes. "Many viral diseases have an incubation period of up to twenty-one days."

My jaw drops open. "You're not keeping us in this room for three weeks."

She smiles as she wraps the tourniquet around my bared arm. "No, no. With most of those diseases you're not contagious until you show symptoms, but since we have no idea what we may be dealing with, we're just getting a good baseline on all of you in case you start to show symptoms later." She inserts the needle painlessly in my puffed-up vein. "Since you, the other officer, and our paramedics were only exposed to the original contact patient before she showed any obvious symptoms, this will only be a twelve-hour observation as a precaution." One tube fills and she inserts a second. "When we release you, we'll transport her to a quarantine facility for further observation. She'll probably have to be quarantined the whole twenty-one days." Second tube filled, she pulls out the needle and staunches the bleeding with a cotton ball then wraps it with purple medical wrap. Now it matches my other arm.

"That sucks. What if the kidnappers were only wearing suits so they didn't leave any evidence behind?"

Her faceplate fogs with a sigh. "Then the city is wasting a whole lot of money, but better safe than an epidemic."

"Sure." My mind is racing. What if they strike again before we can catch them? How many useless quarantines can the city afford? But I guess that's better than the alternative.

CHAPTER 6

Excerpt from Transcript of Session 50:
Dr. Aziz Fritz with Det. S. Harbinger

Fritz: So, you're happy with your new position on the task force.
Harbinger: Of course. Why wouldn't I be?
Fritz: Because it exposes you to WHISPs on a daily basis.
Harbinger: Can't really avoid that now, can I?
Fritz: I mean to say, other people's WHISPs, criminals' WHISPs.
More individuals like Rachel Chester.
Harbinger: She was a unique case.

"DETECTIVE."

I think sleep is an impossibility, but while feigning a nap in an attempt to avoid another heart-to-heart with O'Hea, I fall asleep.

"Hmmm?" Pops of complaint rising from my neck and back, I swing my legs around the side of the cot to the floor. The conference room's harsh overhead fluorescent lights have been turned off, with light coming only from stands brought in by the quarantine team. One of the team, not one I recognize, is standing over me.

"You asked us to notify you when the patient woke up. She's rousing now. I was told that her response to the suits was violent and we're hoping to not have to sedate her again. Dr. Rickerton felt it would be best if she saw a familiar face first."

Rubbing sleep from my eyes, I nod. "Right. Good."

He holds out a mask and protective eyewear like lab glasses. "Just a precaution. She'll still be restrained, but don't get too close."

"Okay."

I make a half-hearted attempt to smooth down my hair before rising and taking the mask and protective glasses. About now, I'm sick of hearing the word precaution. I don the mask and glasses as I walk, and am adjusting the wire over my nose when I reach Isabel's bedside, or gurneyside, as it were. She's moaning softly and writhing beneath her restraints. Under the gurney, her WHISP is an undulating shadow. Something deep within me screams about a monster under the bed, but I ignore that voice. At least, she's no longer wearing her bloody pajamas and robe. I wonder if we'll get them for DNA testing or if the quarantine unit will burn them. I'm debating whether or not to try to wake her when she opens her eyes.

"Hi, Isabel. Remember me? I'm Detective Harbinger. Sylvia. How are you feeling?"

Her eyes go wide with remembrance and she starts thrashing, but at least she's not screaming.

"It's okay, you're safe. You're still at the police station. I didn't let them take you anywhere, but we're worried about you." How much truth can she take? I go for broke. "We think you might have been exposed to something."

She stops struggling. "What?"

"The people who came to take you, they were wearing white suits, right?"

She nods.

"We're afraid they were wearing the suits to protect themselves from a disease or a toxin."

Tears wet the hair at her temples. "Oh God."

"You're not showing any signs of being sick, but we want to make sure. Does that make sense?"

She tries to lift an arm. "Why am I tied down?"

"You were very upset earlier. Some of the doctors here now are wearing white suits like the ones your attackers were wearing. When they came in, they startled you. Do you remember that?"

Closing her eyes, her brows furrowed, she frowns. "Maybe, I don't remember." She opens them again. "Can I see your badge?"

"Of course." I reach into the pocket of my scrubs and pull out my shield and ID (thank goodness I got those back). I hold it close for her to see.

After examining my ID and badge, her head sags against the pillow. "Can you please untie me?"

It doesn't seem like a great idea, and I certainly don't have permission from the quarantine team, but I also think it'll help the interview. "Okay. But there are still doctors here in white suits, so I don't want you to be alarmed. Also, you'll have to be quarantined for a while still. I'm really sorry. There's nothing I can do about that. We need to make sure you're going to be okay."

"Can I call my husband?"

I don't remember seeing a wedding band and she's not wearing one right now. Also, it strikes me as odd that she'd be in a WHISP shelter if she was married, but I want to be on her side for the interview. "Of course. But I'd like to ask you about what happened first."

"He'll see the news. He'll worry."

"If you give me his name, I'll have someone from the precinct contact him and let him know you're all right, but it's very important we talk about what happened right away. The sooner I ask you some questions the better chance you have of remembering something that can help us catch who did this."

She closes her eyes and looks away.

"Please, Isabel. You want to find out who killed your friend, don't you?"

She nods.

"Okay. What's your husband's name?"

"Antonio. Antonio Smith."

"Okay." I pull out my phone to text the Chief. "What's his phone number?"

She tells me and I carefully enter it into the text and check it with Isabel before sending it. Then I start the audio recording app on my phone. "Is that your last name too? Smith?"

She shakes her head. "No. We're separated."

"Is that why you were in the shelter last night?"

She nods.

"How long had you been staying there?"

"Can you untie me now?"

Damn. I was sorta hoping she'd forget about my promise. "Okay, but you have to stay on the gurney and stay calm. All right?"

She nods again and I carefully work the restraint belt off her right wrist. It's not that complicated, but I want everything slow and steady. In fact, I'm half hoping one of the hazmat folks will see what I'm doing and stop me, but they're all oddly inattentive at the moment. When her wrist is free, I tense, waiting for her to lash out at me, but she only wipes her eyes.

"How long had you been staying at the shelter?" I move down to her right leg.

"Only a few days. Antonio was having some trouble adjusting to... We were having some problems and I needed space."

Her leg now free, I wait a beat, but Isabel's body is relaxed and her voice is sad and weary.

"I would've stayed with my sister, but she just had a baby, and I wanted to talk to other people…"

"Like us." I turn to the side, so Liv is visible.

A small smile. "Yeah."

"And you got to know Yosef?" I move around to the other side of the gurney.

She sniffles. "Yeah. He was very nice. He was having a hard time, too. Said he'd lost his job because of his WHISP."

Nodding, I start on the strap on her left leg. If she tries to bolt, it'll be harder to get her left arm free with only one hand than to free her legs with both hands. "Did you notice anything strange at the shelter before last night? Were there any odd visitors or protesters or arguments?"

"No. But I kept in my room or Yosef's room most of the time. I didn't go to the group sessions, but I saw a few others in passing. But they all seemed nice enough."

"None of them seemed scared or worried?"

"Not that I noticed."

Down to the final strap, I take my time even more. "What do you remember from last night?"

Isabel takes a shuddering breath. "It was late, but Yosef and I were up talking. His room is right next to the back door. Sometimes he would go out to the alley and smoke because he wasn't allowed to inside."

"Wait, I thought the back door had an alarm."

"Oh, he'd just slip out quick and put his handkerchief in the slot to keep from getting locked out when he smoked. If you open and close it fast, it doesn't go off."

"There's a delay?"

"Yeah. I think it's so they can take deliveries from the alley sometimes and take out the garbage. It's how I…"—her voice chokes off for a moment—"how I got out that night after…

Yosef was…" With the last strap off, she uses both hands to wipe the tears from her face.

"So, you were both up late talking in his room and then what happened?"

"Then we heard a bang and a commotion at the front of the building. Yosef told me to stay there and crept up to see what was going on. But he didn't come back right away and then I heard him fighting in the hallway with those men."

"How many men? Are you sure they were all men? You didn't hear any women?"

"No women's voices, and I don't know how many men. I just heard shouting and Yosef shouting and I got scared and I… I hid in his trunk. He had one of the big trunks at the end of his bed, but he'd hung up most of his clothes and only kept some cigars in it to keep them moist, so I knew it was empty and I climbed inside, but I could see through a little hole."

"What did you see?"

She swallows hard. "I saw Yosef. He was fighting back against the men in the suits, him and Yonny were. And then one man shouted, 'He's an outlier!' and took out a gun and shot Yosef. They knew he was dead because Yonny went away, and they left him there, but I could still hear them moving around for a while. I was so scared they would notice me missing and come find me, but they didn't. And then, after a long time, I got out and tried to help Yosef even though I knew he was gone. And then I just ran."

An outlier? "Yonny was Yosef's WHISP?"

"Yes."

"How could his WHISP have been fighting back?" The kidnappers in the video didn't have WHISPs and everything I knew told me a WHISP could only hurt another person with a WHISP. If what she was saying about Yosef was true, this could change everything, and not in a good way.

"He was making the lights flicker and throwing things at

the men. Yosef used to like to show me little tricks he could do with Yonny, like have him flip a coin or roll a die."

There's a lump stuck in my throat. "Yonny could move independently of Yosef?"

"Sometimes, but it was hard on Yosef. He had to concentrate. He was very tired afterwards."

"Why didn't you call the police?"

"I just wanted to get out of there. I was afraid they might come back for me. And then I was outside in the cold and Yosef was dead and I couldn't think straight. I just wandered around a long time. Then I found an all-night laundromat and hid in the bathroom and fell asleep. When I woke up, someone was banging on the door and I forgot where I was and when they unlocked the door I ran away again. And then…and then I was here."

"Do you remember anything else about the attack? Did you see any of their faces? Hear any names?"

Isabel's eyes flutter. "No. No faces. They were all wearing those suits and masks."

"Do you remember what they were shouting at Yosef in the hallway?"

"No. I couldn't hear what they were saying until they came inside Yosef's room." A sob escapes her cracked lips. "He could've run out the back door and gotten away, but he was protecting me. I know he was."

"I'm so sorry, Isabel. One last question. Do you know what the man meant by outlier?"

She shakes her head.

CHAPTER 7

Excerpt from Transcript of Session 33:
Dr. Aziz Fritz with Det. S. Harbinger

Fritz: I read Ms. Williams' article in the Times yesterday. Do you want to talk about it?
Harbinger: It's not as bad as some of the things she's written about me.
Fritz: Hers isn't the only article. Have you read any of the others?
Harbinger: I try not to.

AFTER THE INTERVIEW, I SIT AT THE CONFERENCE table gnawing on cold pizza, drinking warm Coke, and trying to picture the attack. We only saw two tranquilizer guns on the video. They must have planned a very quick and efficient snatch and grab: get in while everyone but the desk clerk is asleep, tranq him (now in quarantine somewhere), then move room to room with the tranquilizer guns leading the way, catching everyone blurry-eyed. But they didn't count on Yosef being wide awake and coming to see what was happening or on him being able to fight back with his WHISP. He manages not to get darted and runs back to protect Isabel. They realize he's going to be a problem and shoot him for real. Okay, good theory. Doesn't explain why they didn't realize they missed Isabel. Or maybe they realized their mistake right away and instead of wasting time looking for her, assumed she got out the back and called the police.

Frustration bubbles heart burn up into my throat. Isabel's story explains what happened to Yosef but doesn't explain who was behind the attack, or help us find the other victims. I'm not sure what I was hoping for from her, but something more. Not only am I back at square one, I'm worse than square one because I'm stuck in this freaking conference room. I check my email even though the battery on my cell is at eight percent. *Finally.* There's an email from McCaffrey saying he got the additional footage I'd asked for and that he'll drop it off to me first thing in the morning. I want to tell him I don't care that it's four in the morning, bring it by right now, but I suppose I should be happy he's cooperating, at all.

My phone screams at me again to put it in low power mode and I shut it off and stick it in my pocket. There's a hole in my gut. I glance around the room. Everyone is sleeping or trying to sleep or faking sleep except for three suited figures. Doctors? Possibly. I haven't been paying much attention, but at least some have been doctors. They aren't very chatty. I wonder if they'd notice if I slipped out. Nah. The Chief doesn't mess around. He's probably got someone with a gun watching the other side of the door. Instead, I come up with questions I'll use to grill McCaffrey, like: if CAW's turning over a new leaf, then why are they monitoring WHISP shelters? Their conveniently unhelpful cooperation still rubs me the wrong way. It has to be some kind of smoke screen, right? Get us to spin our wheels on this case while they're off doing something bigger and badder?

Something is nagging the back of my mind, but I can't pin it down. At first, I think it's Yosef's ability to control his WHISP that's bothering me, but, really, I already knew that was possible. The WHISP particles come from their source human, at some point, so it makes sense that there could be some kind of electromagnetic connection. All human thought is electrical impulses, so why couldn't those impulses affect the WHISP particles; condense them, magnetize them so they can interact with solid objects. No, that's not it. My mind strays to Liv sitting in her invisible chair behind me. I try to picture her without seeing her. Try to concentrate and find some kind of connection like Yosef must have done.

My head jerks up from a doze. So much for finding a connection. I check my watch. It's a little after 7 a.m. They should be letting us out any time now. I use the facilities while the paramedics and O'Hea are still snoozing, and use my blank cell screen as a mirror as I comb my fingers through my hair and pick sleepers out of my eyes. It'd be nice to run home for a quick shower, but before I do that I want to meet with McCaffrey when he comes to drop off the video and see if we've gotten anywhere with other city cameras. I've got a spare stick of deodorant in my desk and a spare set of clothes in my locker. That should do until lunch. My stomach growls, but the idea of more leftover pizza doesn't appeal. Would Crone or the Chief think to bring in donuts this morning? Maybe Ben will bring me breakfast. Maybe he's waiting in the lobby of the station right now. I can almost smell his shaving lotion, feel one of his warm hands on my back...

"Morning."

I twitch.

O'Hea's smile wavers. "Sorry, Detective, I didn't mean to startle you."

I force a reciprocal smile. "No, don't worry about it. I just didn't sleep well. And I was dreaming about a breakfast that wasn't pizza."

She sits and glances over at the greasy cardboard boxes. "Yeah. Not sure I could eat anymore either. So, were you able to interview the victim?"

"Yeah, her account answered a few questions but no real leads there."

"Oh. Too bad. I'm sorry."

Shrugging highlights a crick in my neck and I roll my head from side to side. "Me too, but what're ya gonna do?"

O'Hea stifles a yawn and eyes the half-empty two-liter of Coke. I chuckle. "Not the same as coffee, huh?"

"Not even close." She drums her fingers on the table and checks her watch. "They should be letting us go soon, right?"

Glancing over at the white suits near Isabel, I nod. "Think I should go bug them? Maybe they forgot about us or lost track of time." Seems like a good idea, so I stand and head over to the nearest suit. "Hey. Isn't it about that time?"

A thirty-something Asian, maybe Korean, face glares out at me from inside the mask. "We'll let you know, Ma'am."

Don't you Ma'am me. "Might wanna check your records better. No Ma'ams here, only detectives and officers."

His sigh momentarily fogs the clear faceplate. "Sorry"—he glances toward O'Hea at the conference table—"we'll let you know, *Detective.*"

As the idea of smashing his faceplate with my fist flashes through my head, I have to consider if this guy could make my life difficult. Does he really have enough clout to keep me in here longer? Could he mess with my test results? Would his complaint against me lead to a suspension? Something about discretion and valor and not just punching people who piss you off. "Okay. Just don't forget about us." I walk back to the table and O'Hea's mirrored disappointment.

"No luck, huh?"

"Nope." Legs tingling, I brace myself against the table and stretch my cramped muscles.

"I usually do some yoga in the morning."

"Go ahead, nobody's paying attention."

She shakes her head. "These scrubs are too baggy."

"Ah." I finish off by stretching out my arms, then I retrieve my gun and holster from my cot. I want to be ready to take off the minute they let us out of here. My cell buzzes in my pocket, but when I go to answer the call from Ben, the battery dies. "Shit."

"What's wrong?"

"My cell died."

"You want to use mine?"

I weigh the possibility of Ben realizing my phone died versus the possibility he may think something horrible has happened to me. "Yeah, that'd be great. Thanks."

O'Hea hands me hers and I phone Ben back. "Hey babe, I can't talk long. My cell died and I'm using someone else's, but we should be out of here very soon."

"Right. Okay. Well, call back when you're out. Um…have you seen the news?"

"No. Why?"

"Urm, remember that reporter who—"

"What's she done now?"

"Well, apparently you met with someone from CAW again yesterday, um, right after the kidnapping at the WHISP shelter…"

"Oh fuck. How the fuck did she find out about that?"

"I don't know, but there was an exposé this morning on how CAW is now receiving special favors from the NYPD WHISP Task Force which is supposed to be protecting citizens from organizations like CAW, and she called for your suspension from the case. Oh, and also, she mentioned that you were unavailable for comment."

Pain shooting through my jaw tells me I'm grinding my teeth. "Son of a bitch. I'm fucking quarantined!"

Ben clears his throat. "Why are you meeting with CAW again?"

"Argh! It's a long story. They're helping with the investigation...sort of, but it doesn't matter." The blender of my thoughts slows. Maybe CAW leaked the meeting with McCaffrey to get me thrown off the case. But why then would he come back with the other video I asked for? To show more collusion? The damage was already done by the first meeting. Deep breath. It isn't the FBI running the show this time, it's the Chief, and he knew about the meeting. He's not going to throw me off the case, but this will mean the task force will be under a microscope until the kidnapping's solved. Dammit. I could strangle that woman! Hasn't she ever heard of keeping your enemies close?

"Sylvy?"

"I'm still here." Another deep breath. "It's fine. I mean, it's not fine, but it'll be fine. The Chief knew about the meeting, and the task force hadn't even officially been put on the case yet, so, technically, it was just one citizen talking to another citizen. They can't throw me off the case."

"Can't?"

"Won't."

"Okay. Well, I just thought you should know before...if you didn't."

"Yeah, thanks, babe."

Ben sighs through the receiver. "Are you coming home after you get out?"

My heart squeezes. "No. Not right away. Don't wait for me."

"Okay." Translation: There are other people working this case, Sylvy. Shouldn't you lay low for a while?

"Love you. See you and Lincoln tonight."

"Promise."

"Promise." *Probably.*

Excerpt from Transcript of Session 37:
Dr. Aziz Fritz with Det. S. Harbinger

Fritz: It's perfectly normal to mourn the loss of your old life.
Harbinger: But if I do, I'm accepting that things will never be the
same.
Fritz: That's true, isn't it?
Harbinger: Yes, but that doesn't mean I'm ready to accept it.

THE FIRST THING I DO WHEN THEY FINALLY RELEASE us with a sheaf of papers telling us what to do if we cough or sneeze or have a sore throat, is practically run to the locker room, change clothes (do I get to keep these scrubs?), pull the twin bandages from the blood draws off my arms, wash my face, then run my wet fingers through my hair. I also swish and spit a few times for good measure, though the coffee I'm about to grab from the break room will probably mask most of the worst halitosis. Slightly more human now, I breeze by my desk to apply the deodorant then head to the lobby to see if McCaffrey is waiting for me. He isn't. *First thing in the morning, my ass.* Or maybe after seeing the news this morning, he decided not to hand over CAW's other videos. I'll deal with him later.

A few minutes later, with some terrible but hot coffee in hand, I make a second quick stop at my desk, use the extra cable in my desk to plug in my cell, fire up my laptop, then head over to the only other occupied desk. Detective Green usually works the night shift, but I swear she never sleeps. In her forties, she's been a cop for twenty years and a detective for ten of those. She teases me about my almost early retirement. A stalwart, stocky blond with a few inches on me both in height and around the waist, she probably won't retire until a hip gives out.

"Any news?"

Green looks up from her computer, glances around, then checks her watch. "They let you out already?"

"It was just a precaution."

"You look like crap."

"Gee thanks. You spend the night quarantined in a conference room sometime."

She grins. "No thanks. Was it worth it?"

"Worth it?" A flare of anger. *She's not talking about that fucking news story, is she?*

"Did you get anything from the woman from the shelter?"

"Oh. Yes and no." I should probably start writing that report. "She was able to answer some questions we had. But no real leads. Turns out, Yosef was shot because he was awake and fought back. Him and his WHISP."

Green nods. "Another one of those."

Back to business. "Anything on the cameras yet?"

"Well, most of the traffic cams are down—"

"I know, but—"

"—and it's taking time to collect the footage from any possibly useful private cameras." Her brows furrow. "Weren't you supposed to have some other footage for tech to look at?"

I sigh. "Maybe. I—"

My desk phone rings. I abandon Green mid-sentence and head back over to answer it. "Harbinger."

"Detective Harbinger, a Mr. McCaffrey is here to see you."

My eyebrows climb my forehead. *Really?* "Thanks. Can you escort him to an unoccupied interrogation room, please?"

"No problem."

Well, this should be interesting.

Green shouts across the room at me, "You got a lead?"

I shake my head. "Probably not. But someone I do want to chew a new asshole."

"Ah. Have fun."

I check my cell. It's only at two percent, so I leave it, but grab my coffee, and, not bothering to wait for the elevator, hit the stairs. Upstairs, there's only one interrogation room door closed, but I still check the observation room next door, mainly for the sick satisfaction of peeking through the two-way glass at Rondell McCaffery. He's wearing grey pants today with a green button-down shirt and matching patterned sweater vest. A heavy grey wool pea coat hangs over the suspect chair, but he's up and pacing. Slightly less laid back today. Good. Or maybe it's just the difference between the unofficial air of the conference room versus the big brother air of the interrogation room.

I'd like to sip my bad coffee and let him sweat a while longer, but if there's any worth to the video he's brought, my indulgence could cost lives. When I enter the room, he shoots me a look, his face a mass of irritation.

"I thought we had a deal, Detective."

I sit and place my coffee on the desk, hand hovering over the recording button for a moment. Wouldn't be admissible unless I told him I was recording, but still tempting. "I don't know why you would think that."

Incredulity replaces irritation. "Oh, come on. We give you crucial evidence and you turn around and screw us with it?"

"If you're talking about the news report, I haven't seen it, but I'm given to understand that the NYPD and I are the ones looking like assholes."

"Haven't seen it? Where've you been all morning?"

I shouldn't tell him about the quarantine. If CAW's responsible, I don't want to give them any feedback into how their plan is going, but at the same time, I want to rattle McCaffrey's cage and judge his reaction. "In quarantine, actually."

"I— Wait, what?"

To his credit, he appears genuinely confused. He must've known about the lock down of the crime scene, but he also knows I'd never been there. It doesn't mean he didn't know about the kidnapping or a bioweapon, just means he can't figure out how I would've been exposed to it. But now I have to decide how to explain my exposure without telling him about Isabel. "I went to see the body at the coroner's office and my containment suit had a hole in it."

McCaffrey takes in my appearance again: rumpled clothes, no makeup, frizzy hair, dark circles under the eyes. "Oh."

"So, I'm sorry about the bad press, but I was, as they said, unavailable for comment."

"Um. Are you…is everything…"

"It was just a precaution." Precious time is wasting. "Can I have the additional footage now?"

Nodding, he steps over to the other chair and reaches into his coat pocket, this time pulling out a memory stick. He holds it out to me. "Each file is titled with the name of the shelter and the date. I was able to pull the past two weeks of the three licensed shelters in the city, but I don't think the videos are going to be of much help."

I take the stick. "Why do you say that?"

"We've also had people examining the video. If the shelters

were cased before Tuesday night, they didn't use a white van, and we didn't see anything unusual."

"We'll see." I want to run up to tech with this, but I'm not quite through with McCaffrey. "If CAW truly is turning over a new leaf, why are they monitoring WHISP shelters?"

McCaffrey finally sits. "To make sure CAW members aren't protesting or vandalizing them."

I scoff, but his face remains neutral. "Wait, you're serious?"

"Like I said, we're taking a new direction. We can't do anything about people who already have WHISPs, so we're refocusing on prevention. Calling for less exposure of children to ambient and waste radiation, magnetism, and radio waves, encouraging parents to limit their own and their kids' use of smartphones, looking into better shielding methods of microwaves and cell towers, that sort of thing."

I want to believe him, but I also live in the real world. "Why did you join CAW, Rondell?" A nicer question than: How does a grease monkey become a CAW spokesperson?

"Because I don't think WHISPs are a natural phenomenon. They're not healthy, and you know as well as I do that they can be dangerous."

"People can be dangerous. Life can be dangerous."

"Yeah, but this is a danger we can prevent. For everyone to just accept WHISPs without seeing them as a symptom of an ailing society is crazy. There is nothing good about them."

He's not wrong. If the need for WHISP shelters proves anything, it's that WHISPs are altering many people's lives for the worst. But there's something else. "Do you have any family members with WHISPs?"

Rondell winces.

There it is.

"A brother."

"Something happen?"

His response comes through clenched teeth. "He had a

WHISP, he couldn't cope, he killed himself."

And you think joining CAW is a way to honor his memory? "I'm sorry."

His eyes are red, but dry. "I don't want any more people to have to go through what I did. What other people are having to go through. Parents of bullied kids with WHISPs, people whose spouses have left them, who've lost their jobs, it could all be prevented. I'm not against people with WHISPs, I'm against people getting WHISPs in the first place."

"I'm not sure CAW shares your views. You could've started your own organization or joined a WHISP support group."

"CAW is the largest and most well-funded. I didn't want to try to compete with them for money, and most of those other groups focus on what to do after the fact, how to cope or WHISP solidarity, not prevention."

"If CAW turns out to be responsible for this, how are you going to feel about them then? Still going to want to be a member?"

He stands. "Of course not. But we aren't." He grabs his coat. "Maybe you should stop wasting time harassing me and find out who *was* responsible." He makes for the door then turns. "Do your job, Detective. I would think you, of all people, would want to find out who did this." He leaves.

I let him go. Me of all people? Because of my WHISP? It's a stupid, weak parting shot, but forces me to resist the urge to look in the mirror as I exit. At least now, I know I'm not going to get anything more from CAW through McCaffrey. He's too emotionally invested and totally in the dark with regards to what CAW is really all about. If they are involved, he has no idea. The perfect person to send to the NYPD as a representative.

On my way to deliver the memory stick to tech, Green finds me.

"I'm headed out, but tech finally has a lead on the white van from a private camera. I told them you'd be right up."

"Thanks."

Taking the stairs two at a time, I'm sweating when I burst into their department. There are a few people at their desks now that it's a little after eight. They all look up, but it's a towheaded kid who looks like he should be surfing the California waves instead of the internet who motions me over. I've seen him around, but never spoken to him. His name's Pzyckski or Polesky; something Polish. Without introducing himself, he points to his screen, which is filled with the image of a fuzzy, white van.

"This is from the front door of an apartment complex over on Avenue D. It was captured about five minutes from the time of the abduction, which tracks the transit time from the shelter." He zooms out. "And here."

A partial license plate comes into view and I want to kiss him. Instead, I scribble the digits and letter down on a sticky note from his desk. "Nice work. Were they heading north or south?"

He nods. "South."

"Can you get any angle on the driver or spot anything else helpful?"

"No, but now that we know the direction, it narrows the search area considerably. I should have more for you soon."

"Excellent. Thanks, um…"

"Polanski, Brian."

"Thanks, Polanski." I turn to go, then remember the memory stick in my hand. "This is more footage of the shelter from earlier in the week and surveillance from the other WHISP shelters in the city. Should I give this to you, or…" I glance around the room.

"I'll take it. You're hoping to see something suspicious prior to the kidnapping?"

"Exactly."

CHAPTER 9

Excerpt from Transcript of Session 43:
Dr. Aziz Fritz with Det. S. Harbinger

*Fritz: I think your fear is perfectly rational. You said Chester
could only attack other WHISPers, so it would make sense that
you feel more exposed now that you have a WHISP.*
*Harbinger: I don't think that's it, at least, not all of it. I am
afraid of other people's WHISPs, but I think I'm more afraid…*
Fritz: Afraid of your own? In what way?
Harbinger: It's stupid.
Fritz: I'm listening.
Harbinger: What if it turns on me?

I'M HEADING DOWNSTAIRS TO RUN THE PLATE WHEN
the stairwell spins and I miss a step, landing hard on my ass
and sloshing coffee on my pants. *Whoa, what was that?* Must be
low blood sugar despite the two packets I dumped into my
coffee. Holding the rail for support, I stand and wait for my
head to float away again. When it doesn't, I continue down a
little slower and rip open a power bar from my desk before
starting the plate search. I don't know whether the bar is bad

or whether my stomach is still upset from pizza in the middle of the night, but just as I enter in the fourth of the four characters, the bar comes back up.

Grabbing the trashcan as I spit hunks of partially digested bar into it, I hear someone clear their throat next to me.

"Go home, Harbinger."

I wipe my mouth with some tissues from the box on my desk. "I'm fine. Really. I think it was that pizza from last night. We got a break on the van. Polanski caught the van on a private surveillance camera and got a partial plate."

The Chief sighs. "I know. He texted me, too. I'll get Harris to run it."

I point to my computer. "But I'm running it now."

"Harbinger, no one appreciates your work ethic like I do, but you were in quarantine all night, have a coffee stain on your pants, could really use a shower, and just puked up your breakfast. This isn't a request. We'll let you know as soon as we track down the van's owner."

All the arguments about how time-sensitive kidnappings are and how I can shower in the locker room die on my lips in the face of the Chief's expression: *we need you at your best on this one.* I know that's especially true because of my meeting with McCaffrey and the whole media shitstorm. The sour taste in my mouth isn't just from the vomit. I nod. "Okay."

His shoulders relax but his face is still tight. "Good. Get a shower, get some rest, there's nothing more you can do right now." He turns to leave, then turns back. "Are you sure you're feeling okay?"

"I'm fine, little heartburn, that's all."

His eyes stray to the trashcan, but he doesn't say anything more.

Resisting the urge to check how the plate search is coming along, I chuck my empty coffee cup in the trash, pack up my laptop, and put on my coat. I'm about to pocket my cell when I remember that I haven't called Ben to let him know I'm out. *Crap.* I send him a quick text.

Sylvy: I'm free! Headed home for a shower and a nap. Kiss emoji.

———

I HIT A WALL ALMOST AS SOON AS I GET BACK TO Lincoln's apartment and shovel some cold cereal in my face before collapsing on the guest bed. When I awaken to cramps and a growling stomach, the clock reads 2:22 p.m. *Oh crap.* My internal clock is going to be ruined for days. Reflexively, I reach for my cell. There's an email from Green.

Green: Plate's a bust. Van was stolen about four weeks ago from a rental agency. No Lowjack. Frowny face.

Shit, shit, shit. I shoot off a reply.

Harbinger: Thanks. Check with Polanski in tech. He's tracking van + working additional footage city shelters.

It's fine. The plate would've been too easy. But maybe I should check out the rental agency and see if any CAW members ever rented from there or worked there. My stomach grumbles again. *After lunch.* As I stand, the distinct smell of sour sweat wafts over me. *Lunch and a shower.*

I shuffle out in my sweats and find Ben on a laptop at the kitchen table. Seeing me, he leaps up and sweeps me into his arms.

"How are you feeling?"

Annoyance surges through me, bolstered by the crankiness of having just woken up, but I bite back my initial response: *Shouldn't you be at work?* "I'm fine. What're you doing here?"

Ben loosens the hug so he can look at me. His face isn't hiding a touch of hurt feelings. "I wanted to see you. I called the station to see if I could bring you some food and the Chief said he'd ordered you to go home."

Didn't he get my text? I glance at his computer and the words just slip out, "I'm not staying. I have to get back."

The hurt in Ben's face deepens, but there's no taking back my comment. He drops his arms to his sides and tries to smile. "Oh. Big break in the case?"

I'm not sure I'd classify spotting the van on tape and having the plate turn into a dead-end a break, but it's not nothing. "Sort of. You know how crucial time is with kidnapping cases."

"Right. Sure." He turns to the fridge. "Can I fix you something?"

I sit across from his computer at the tiny kitchen table. "A sandwich?"

He surveys the contents of the refrigerator. "Ham okay?"

"Sure." I want to make some coffee too, but both of us trying to make food in Lincoln's one-butt kitchen would lead to disaster.

"So, what was the quarantine like?"

"Oh, you know, boring with a lot of blood drawing."

With the bread, mayonnaise, and ham now on the counter, Ben closes the fridge and starts on sandwich assembly. "Still don't have any idea what they're looking for?"

"No. And the witness, Isabell, isn't showing any symptoms of exposure to anything. More than likely, they were wearing the suits to minimize identification and trace evidence. And it worked, because Isabel couldn't give me any descriptions."

"Was she able to tell you anything useful? How'd she get away?"

"She hid and then ran out the back after the kidnappers left. Turns out her friend Yosef was killed trying to protect her... with his WHISP."

Ben slides the sandwich in front of me. "Oh?"

"Yeah, she said he'd learned to make it do tricks like flip coins and throw dice. I guess he was using it to throw things at the kidnappers and they got scared and shot him for real."

In the process of sitting, Ben stands again. "Do you want some coffee or—"

"Coffee, please."

He smiles, dumps the dregs, and starts making a new pot. Then pauses. "Why did you say, 'shot him for real?'"

Sometimes I really do forget that Ben isn't privy to all my cases. "The kidnappers had tranquilizer guns. Looks like most of the victims were sedated before being moved. He was the only one shot with a bullet."

The coffee brewing, Ben turns. "Those suits have pockets on the outside?"

I have to swallow a large bite of ham, bread, and condiment before answering, "I don't know. Why?"

He has his calculating-something face on now. "Well, you said they had tranquilizer guns when they went in and that you didn't see any regular guns."

"Right."

"Well, if they didn't have the regular guns in pockets on the outside of the suits then—"

"Then they'd have to have had them underneath their suits—"

"Meaning they'd have had to open their suits."

My heart's racing. "Or, at least, one of them did." I'm straining to remember the exact words Isabel used when she described Yosef's shooting. I think she said one of the men 'took out' a gun and shot him, but I didn't think to ask where he'd taken it out from. "Which would've been really stupid if they'd just tested a bioweapon or toxin in the shelter." It didn't get us any closer to finding the kidnapping victims, but it would make the investigation much easier if we didn't have to set up quarantines every five minutes.

"Unless..." The grin on Ben's face has collapsed. His gaze flits behind me, then to me again.

"Unless what?"

"None of the kidnappers had WHISPs, right?"

"Right. Makes sense. I assume they're an anti-WHISP group." I roll my eyes and shake my head. "Possibly CAW." I take another bite.

"Well, it might be possible..."—the gears behind his eyes whirl and turn—"that whatever they were testing only affects individuals with WHISPs."

My whole body freezes up, mouth open in mid-chew, Ben's words slowly sinking into my brain. *It wasn't possible, was it?* Abruptly the quarantine takes on all new connotations. With difficulty, I swallow. "How could it..."

He's not looking at me or the kitchen, now. He's staring into his research, pouring over thoughts and theories. "It would have to be some kind of particle disruption or effect the electrical impulses or electrochemistry of the brain. There are certain viruses that depolarize muscle cells and degenerative diseases in the brain can disrupt electrical impulses, but for those to only affect WHISPs, it would have to be a reverse feedback, not from the human, but from the WHISP. Something that changed the particle outside the body and sent it back into the body corrupted, or sent some sort of damaging feedback into the body or the brain." He finally refocuses. "I'm not sure exactly how it would work, but I think it could be done."

One phrase sticks out: *sent some sort of damaging feedback*. Like the feedback Chester's WHISP sent her when I destroyed it in the particle accelerator. WHISP and human are linked; hurt the WHISP, hurt the human. "Why wouldn't they just use something like an EMP?" Like I'd tried and failed to use in the pathetic trap I'd laid for Chester.

"Something like that would risk causing more WHISPs, particularly to the people using it."

Numb, I nod. "Could something like that have a time delay?"

Ben shakes his head, but then hesitates. "Not something directly working on the WHISP particles probably, but…"

"But what?"

"Well, if it were something with a feedback loop between the person and the WHISP, then maybe."

"What do you mean by feedback loop?"

Ben pushes off the counter and paces the few allowable steps. "If the reaction, whatever it was, started in the human, was transferred to the WHISP particles, and then back to the human, then there might be a delay between infection and symptoms. Like…like a wave hitting a break wall and bouncing back, or vibrations rebounding along a bridge until it collapses."

"But those are waves, not particles."

He stops pacing. "Particles can sometimes act like waves."

Reigning in terror, I shake my head. Occam's Razor. "But this is far-fetched, right? I mean, the far more likely explanation is that the kidnappers were trying to avoid identification and leaving trace evidence."

"Right."

But I can tell he's not done with this and it'd be reckless to dismiss the idea entirely. I find Ben's eyes. "You should call the Chief, tell him your theory."

"It's not a theory, just a…a possibility."

"Even so." Rubbing my forehead, heat meets my fingertips. Panic jumpstarts my heart; tingles run down my spine. Stop. Relax. It's just your blood sugar spiking from the sandwich. I regard the half still left on my plate, once so appetizing, now an unappealing slab, but I force another bite. I don't want to get into another hunger desperation situation like the one that probably caused me to puke earlier. *What if it wasn't the bar? No, this is crazy.* Also, "But how would something like that be contagious?"

Ben has his cell out, presumably about to take my advice,

but hasn't pressed send yet. "The same way as any other disease, really. It depends on the catalyst of the feedback loop, but if the suits really were for protection, I'd guess airborne...unless..."

"Unless what?"

He doesn't meet my gaze. "Unless they found a way to pass it WHISP to WHISP, more like a prion."

"A prion?" I vaguely recognize the word. I'm pretty sure it's connected to Mad Cow Disease.

"It's a protein that affects other proteins and causes them to fold differently. It's the culprit behind Scrapie in sheep and Kuru in humans, where proteins in the brain are affected. This would be infected WHISP particles affecting other WHISP particles."

At first, I want to remind Ben that a person's WHISP particles don't interact with other people's WHISP particles, but Chester's WHISP could only directly kill other people with WHISPs. "Oh." *Oh shit.*

Excerpt from Transcript of Session 52:
Dr. Aziz Fritz with Det. S. Harbinger

Fritz: You seem distracted today.
Harbinger: Lincoln and I had a fight.
Fritz: That's not surprising. You two haven't lived in such close quarters since he became an adult. It would be a difficult situation for any parent and child, and especially difficult for you when you're still trying to repair your relationship with him.
Harbinger: He said I was still a WHISP bigot. Said I was the worst kind of WHISP bigot because I hated myself.
Fritz: Do you?
Harbinger: Hate myself? ...Sometimes.

EVER SINCE BEN BROUGHT UP THE POSSIBILITY OF A WHISP only, WHISP-transmitted disease, the tug of Liv on my back has gotten stronger, almost like an itch I can't reach. Even the shower feels crowded. Gone are the sweet moments of forgetfulness when people aren't giving me odd or repulsed looks. I keep telling myself that I'm overreacting, but then I recall helping Isabel into the conference room and my WHISP's arm under her WHISP's arm. How close did Yosef's WHISP get to hers while she was hiding in that trunk? Where did his WHISP's particles go when he died, and how fast? Isabel wasn't showing any symptoms, but what if she started to? Would I need to go into quarantine, again?

Oh my God, Lincoln. Should I even go back to the apartment?

Despite an open policy, there aren't that many cops in our precinct with WHISPs and I'm the only one on the task force other than Lincoln, so avoidance shouldn't be too big a problem. Still, I feel like a typhoid Mary when I walk into the precinct. Quickly descending into the basement, I almost trip myself checking over my shoulder. The tension only eases slightly when I reach my desk. Maybe I shouldn't be here, but the Chief didn't tell me to stay home, and what else am I supposed to do? I suppose I should be happy I wasn't ambushed with another quarantine when I walked through the door.

My computer hasn't finished booting when the Chief comes over. He attempts a smile. "Harbinger. You look better. How are you feeling?"

The lightest feather brushes between my shoulder blades. "Fine. Better. I got a nap, lunch and shower."

He nods and clears his throat. "Until we get everything sorted, I'm going to have to ask you to be on restricted duty."

Anger bubbles up in my chest, but it could be worse. He could order me into quarantine. "Right."

"Until further notice, we're putting the task force into lockdown. No one not a member of this department comes into the department."

"Okay."

"And I have to ask you to stay in the department while you're here at the station."

I swallow. "Okay."

His shoulders droop a fraction of an inch. "I'm sorry." He sighs. "Do you have some place to stay tonight?" He knows me and my family and our current living situation.

I try to think of a place where I know I'd be able to avoid contact with other WHISPs. Nothing comes immediately to mind. "I...I'll talk to Ben and Lincoln. Maybe Lincoln can stay with a friend."

The Chief nods. "Well, I'll leave you to it then." He walks back to his office.

Leave me to what, exactly? I check my e-mail and there's a message from Green with the subject heading 'van.' I glance across to her vacant desk before opening it.

Green: Have a search area for the van. Will keep you updated.

I see an email from Polanski, as well, with CCs to the whole task force.

Polanski: Couldn't find another shot of van even though it should've passed by a working traffic cam. I'd recommend canvasing between cameras.

The message from Polanski is time stamped from around 2:45 p.m., and the one from Green is from 3:30 p.m. It's nearing four, so Green and the rest of the team haven't been out long. Still, the ache of exclusion is real. I reply to Polanski and ask him about the footage I got from McCaffrey this morning. If he'd found something worthwhile, I'm sure he'd have emailed already, but it gives me something to do. Then I decide to review the recording of my interview with Isabel. I'd already relayed the highlights, but I'm still curious about her wording with regards to where the gun came from that shot Yosef. It might be important in whether they have to quarantine the van when they find it. I might need to interview her again over the phone, but it'll take time to track down where she's been moved to and how to request another interview.

Unfortunately, after replaying the interview, I'm right that

Isabel only said the attackers 'took out' a gun. I ping the Chief with a text to find out where she's been taken. He replies within seconds that she's at Bellevue Hospital in the infectious disease ward. I call the hospital and am transferred three times before reaching the ward Isabel is in, only to have the nurse tell me she's sleeping, but she'll call me as soon as she's awake. Since I'm calling on the station's land line, the receiver makes a satisfying noise when I slam it down.

Less than ten seconds later, it rings and I jump. "Harbinger."

"It's Green. We found the van."

That was quick. "And?"

"It's been dumped. Kidnappers definitely switched vehicles on us."

"Shit. Any tire tracks?"

Green sighs through the phone. "No. The van's in an alley between two abandoned buildings but the asphalt's pretty clean."

"Had to be a vehicle at least as large as a van though, right?"

"Presumably."

"I'll get Polanski, or whoever's taking over for him on the night shift, to continue checking the video for a van or truck headed the same direction as the van about ten minutes after the van disappeared."

"Okay, but they could've doubled back to throw us off."

I tap my chin with the forefinger of my left hand. "I don't think so. I mean, if this was as planned as we think it was with regards to half the traffic cams being out and the swapped vehicles, I think they're probably going to rely on that to avoid detection, don't you? If I were them, I'd pick a route that avoided all working traffic cams and trust in that."

"I guess, but maybe they weren't sure which cameras were going to be out."

"Since the city definitely didn't advertise that any were going to be out, I have to assume the kidnappers hacked in and knew which ones."

"Hmm, a hack you say?"

I sit up in my chair. "Right, of the city's road department files. I'll get tech on it. You processing the van on site?"

"No, we have to move it somewhere secure in case it's plague-ridden or whatever. Just a precaution, but I almost wish we didn't have that video of the kidnappers in their hazmat suits."

I'm sure Green has heard about Ben's theory through the Chief, but I don't bring it up. It's possible everyone without a WHISP is safe, but we don't know anything for certain. "Right, well, see you when you get back."

"Sure."

I press down the receiver then pick it right back up and call the cybercrime division of tech.

"Lewiston."

"Hey, this is Detective Harbinger from the WHISP Task Force. We think the city's road department files pertaining to the traffic cam shutdown this week may have been hacked."

"Okay."

"You'll check into it."

"I've got quite a few other cases in the queue, but I'll get to it by Monday, maybe."

"This is a kidnapping case."

"Oh, sorry, Detective. I'll call you as soon as I have something."

"Thanks. I appreciate it."

Maybe the only good thing about kidnapping cases is that everyone knows they're time critical.

———

AROUND SIX, AFTER CALLING THE RENTAL AGENCY the van came from and being promised a list of recent customers as well as recent employees, and getting Sekibo from tech to follow up on possible second kidnapper vehicles caught on camera, I call Ben.

"Hey."

"Hey you, how's the case?"

"We found the van, but it'd been dumped."

"That sucks."

"Yep."

"You coming home tonight?" A not-so-subtle hint.

"Probably. There's not much I can get done here. I've been relegated to partial duty. Um, have you talked to Lincoln about...things?"

"Yeah. He's going to stay with his friend Naomi tonight."

The mother in me wants to ask more about this Naomi, but this isn't the time. *How long will I have to avoid my own son?* "Does he have any other thoughts about your theory?" *Did he shoot it down as impossible?* Fingers crossed.

"No. We're both in agreement that it's possible, but since we can only do computer modelling of WHISP particle behavior experiments at this point, it's hard to say how." A pause. "So, will you be home soon? Can I make you dinner?"

I want to say no. I want to have something I can do, some lead I need to follow, but this case is one frustrating dead end after another. There's a slight chance the hospital will call and let me talk to Isabel, but in all honesty, that can wait until tomorrow, and even if tech is able to track a suspicious vehicle that could be the second vehicle, I'm not going to be the one to follow up on it in the field. I've been frustrated on cases before, but I'm not sure I've ever felt this useless. "Yeah. I'm just going to finish up a little paperwork here, then I'll be on my way."

"Spaghetti?"

One of Ben's go-to dinner offerings. "Sounds good."

I survey the department. Yong and Diwan are the only two at their desks and I wonder if Green's coming back. Maybe she handed off van detail to Yong. I find Lewiston's email and tell him to call Diwan instead of me with any results and to email any updates to the task force group email. Sekibo will already know to do that. Then I do finish up a bit of paperwork, making it a little after six-thirty when I finally grab my coat and laptop and head up the stairs. In the stairwell, I pause to text the Chief that I'm leaving so he can lift the department lock down. I meet Green on her way down.

"Headed out?"

"Unless you have something I can help with?"

She grins. "Paperwork on the van?"

"Tempting, but I think I'll pass."

"Suit yourself."

She passes and a jealousy for her paperwork does well up in me. She's moving the case forward and I'm going home for spaghetti. I should hate these bastard kidnappers just because they're bastard kidnappers praying on people trying to get away from WHISP hate and find solace and understanding, because they murdered a fifty-eight year old man in cold blood, and because maybe they're toying with lives by inventing some kind of new bioweapon. But right now, I hate them most because I'm on the sidelines. It's messed up yet true. I decide to blame my skewed ire on having to deal with the scum of the earth, or, at least, the city, for over thirty years.

———

AFTER DINNER, BEN AND I TAKE ADVANTAGE OF Lincoln's absence to snuggle on the couch and watch a few of our favorite streaming media shows. It's a lovely evening, and I'm miserable and checking my email every five minutes until Ben finally breaks. He pauses the show.

"Sylvy, I know this is a kidnapping case, but you've got a whole task force working with you and you're the day shift. Let the night shift do their job. You don't need to do everything yourself anymore."

He's not wrong, but his comment gets my dander up anyway. "So, you're okay with me lounging around while these people are possibly tortured or experimented on? What if it was Lincoln?"

Ben pulls away. "Don't do that. If there was something that only you could do and you weren't doing it, that would be one thing. But what can you possibly do tonight to help this case? Are there leads you haven't told me about? Even if there are, what are you going to do about them when you're confined to the precinct? In fact, the Chief wanted you…" He looks away.

"What? The Chief wanted me what?"

"He wanted to take you off the case because of the chance of there being an agent that only affects WHISPs."

"We don't know that."

He faces me. "It's a real possibility, Sylvy. Shit, you may have already been exposed to something."

"I'm fine."

"I hope to Christ that you are, and I told the Chief not to pull you from the case, but Sylvy, can you understand that this isn't just about you? What if Lincoln had come home with me to see you before we figured out what might be going on?"

Now who's bringing Lincoln into this? "It's not my fault that woman ended up at our precinct."

"I never said it was. It's just, sometimes you get so involved in a case… Listen, I'm supporting you, I've always supported you, and I'll continue to support you, but every victim is not your personal responsibility."

My throat is too tight to speak. Stupid rage throbs in my temples. Ben is right. Not only is he right, but what right do I have to feel personally responsible for these people? I've been so caught up with tracking down the kidnappers that I haven't even bothered to check if we've gotten the victims' names released from the shelter yet. Still, I can't apologize.

Ben leans in for a hug and my first reaction is to push him away, but I let him hug me without hugging back. He pulls back, but not away. "Do you want me to sleep on the couch?"

I snort. "This isn't funny."

"I know. But I'm worried about you."

I'm fine. The words die on my lips. I'm not fine. Not even close to fine, and, oh yeah, my WHISP might be some kind of ticking time bomb. "Okay."

"Okay that I'm worried or okay, you can sleep on the couch?"

"A little of both, but you don't have to sleep on the couch."

CHAPTER 11

Excerpt from Transcript of Session 58:
Dr. Aziz Fritz with Det. S. Harbinger

Fritz: So, this is about identity?
Harbinger: Yes.
Fritz: Can you elaborate?
Harbinger: I've been a cop almost half my life. I'm a cop, that's who I am. Okay, maybe a woman cop, but still, a cop, a detective. I know how to be that. But people don't see me as that anymore. They only see my WHISP. Now I'm a WHISPer who happens to be a cop.
Fritz: Are you talking about just the public or at work, too?
Harbinger: It's the worst at the precinct. Some cops I went through training with now look at me like I don't know what I'm doing, like my WHISP somehow sucked out my cop abilities.
Fritz: Have you tried talking to them about it?
Harbinger: That'd make it worse. It's not how cops deal with things.

THE NEXT MORNING, I HAVEN'T DIED AND, IN THE bathroom mirror, Liv looks about the same as always. I force myself to wait until after I've showered and dressed to check my email. Sipping coffee and nibbling on a bagel, I nearly choke when I open the attachment from the rental agency with a list of recent employees and customers. One customer name jumps off the screen: Rondell McCaffrey. *Son of a bitch!* Leaving Ben in the shower, I'm out the door roughly a minute later and then at the station another twenty minutes after that. It's not quite enough evidence for a warrant, but it is enough to bring him in for questioning.

I'm still on partial duty, even though the hospital called last night and left a message that Isabel would be able to talk to me later that day, meaning she was still showing no symptoms. Also, because of the news story claiming CAW was getting special treatment from the NYPD, I'm coordinating with the Chief how we want to proceed with McCaffrey when another bombshell drops. Forensics found a single fingerprint in the van and guess whose shoplifting record it matches? Now we have plenty for a warrant. I'm only sad I won't be there when they make the arrest.

While I wait for uniforms to bring him in and officially book him on suspicion of kidnapping, I prepare myself for the interview and check with tech on the city files hack, and to see if they've had any luck tracking the kidnappers' second vehicle. Nothing yet on the hack, but they're chasing down a few possible van and truck leads. The day is getting better and better, especially after the Chief clears Green and me to conduct the interview.

McCaffrey, in a disheveled green cardigan and khakis, is pacing when we enter the interrogation room. "This is a mistake. I told you I had nothing to do with that kidnapping, Detective."

"Mr. McCaffrey, this is Detective Green. Please sit down." We both take a seat, but McCaffrey shakes his head.

"No. This is insane. Why am I here? Because of the footage? That could've come from anyone. This is harassment of CAW."

I look to Green and she takes out a copy of a receipt from a file and lays it on the table.

"No, it isn't. This is a copy of a receipt for a rental car from Speedy Rentals with your name on it."

McCaffrey glances down at the paper. "Yeah, so? I needed a car to attend a WHISP-prevention rally in New Jersey, so what?"

Green raises a single eyebrow. "So, this is the same company from which the van used in the WHISP shelter kidnapping was stolen."

He frowns. "That's just a coincidence."

Green continues, "Then I suppose it is also 'just a coincidence' that your fingerprint was found in the van the kidnappers used."

"What?" McCaffrey's face clouds. "That's impossible."

My turn. "Not if you accidentally touched the door after you removed your hazmat suit."

"No. No, that's crazy. This is crazy. I had nothing to do with this." He finally sits and takes a deep breath. "I want a lawyer."

Ah, the "L" word. With the interview officially over, Green rises. "You're gonna need one."

I follow Green, but pause at the door and turn back to McCaffrey. "You had me convinced, you know. The story about your brother and CAW turning over a new leaf." I shake my head. "I admit, you had me."

"It wasn't me. It wasn't CAW." He seems sincere enough.

"The evidence says otherwise."

He shakes his head. "I'm being framed. CAW's being framed."

"By who? Why?"

"I don't know who, but we're an easy scapegoat."

Possibly. "Why you then?"

"I'm the new face of CAW. I'm the one spearheading our changes. They want to keep us an evil entity."

"Again. Who's they?"

He looks away and shrugs. "That's your job."

A little push. "If you are involved, Rondell, I could help you. If you tell us where those people are, I could talk to the DA. Make a deal."

He slams an open palm down on the table and stares back at me. "I had nothing to do with it. We're done."

I nod. "Okay."

As I exit, Green comes out of the observation room. "It was a good angle, too bad he didn't take the offer."

I tug at my lower lip. The kidnapping should've been CAW, but from the onset, CAW was supposedly trying to help us solve the case. Now, all the evidence neatly points to CAW. I don't like it. "Yeah, too bad."

———

Green and I sit at the small table in the corner of the basement next to the coffee pot that passes for the task force's break room, digging into an order of Chinese food that arrived about five minutes ago.

"Do you think CAW will throw him under the bus?" Green asks.

"Huh?"

Green waves her chopsticks around. "McCaffrey. Do you think they'll say he organized the whole thing on his own and try to deny their involvement?"

"That'd be the smart thing to do. I guess it all depends on what we find at his home and office, and how much shredding and hiding they can do between now and then, but they risk him flipping on them if they do." I just manage to pick up a dumpling and put it in my mouth before it slips from my chopsticks.

"He seems like a wheelman to me."

Between chews of beef-cilantro goodness, "Is that where they found the print?"

"Yep."

I swallow. "Huh. Just his print."

"Clear as day. On the back of the top of the steering wheel. Must've gotten sloppy wiping it down. Or touched it after they wiped it down."

"Touched the back of the steering wheel after wiping it down?"

Green pauses in shoveling brown rice into her mouth. "You don't believe his bullshit story about being framed, do you?"

No? "If he was sloppy with his bare hands after wiping things down, then you'd expect more than one of his prints. You don't grab a wheel with one finger. And if he was just a sloppy wiper, wouldn't there be overlapping prints from other drivers? It is a rental van, after all."

"I—"

"And why wipe it down at all? You know you're going to dump it, you're already wearing a hazmat suit, so why not keep it on until you're in the second vehicle? No fuss, no muss?"

Green gives me a "really" look. "Maybe he got hot in the suit, or couldn't see the road to drive, or didn't put the suit on until they got there and then forgot to wipe down the wheel. Who knows? Point is, we got lucky."

"Why would CAW steal a van from a rental place they frequent? That seems pretty stupid."

"Or smart. They knew the layout of the place, knew what vehicles they had available, when the lot would be empty."

"Maybe." As I pop another dumpling into my mouth, my cell phone buzzes. It's Lewiston from Tech. "Harbinger."

"Detective, I found that hack into the city road files and was able to trace it."

My whole body tenses. "And?"

"It traced back to an IP address at the CAW New York headquarters."

"You're kidding."

"Nope."

Well, so much for that.

———

WHILE WAITING TO HEAR THE RESULTS OF THE search warrants, I call the hospital for the second interview with Isabel. From a number left by the nurse, I get her direct room line.

"Hello?"

"Isabel, this is Detective Harbinger."

"Oh yes, Detective. They said you'd call."

"How are you feeling?"

"To be honest, a little claustrophobic."

I chuckle. "I remember that feeling. I'm only sorry yours has to be so long."

"Thank you. Um, what can I help you with?"

"I wanted to ask you a few more follow-up questions about the night Yosef was murdered."

She sucks in a deep breath. "All right."

"When you said that the men in suits took out a gun and shot him, where did they take the gun from?"

"What do you mean?"

"Was it from say, a pocket on the outside of the suit or a holster or did the man unzip his suit?"

"Oh, um, I think he unzipped it."

"You think?"

She pauses. "It all happened so fast. And sometimes one of

them was in front of the trunk, blocking my view, and it was hard to tell what was going on because everything was upside down."

"Upside down?"

"Well, I had to lay on my back in the trunk. Otherwise, they might've seen my WHISP."

"Oh right." *Would I have thought of that in her situation?* Probably not. But it's possible she's had her WHISP longer than I have.

"Anything else?"

"Was Yonny acting strange or did he look strange when Yosef was fighting with the men?"

"Strange how?"

No idea. "A different color maybe or maybe a little more dispersed or transparent or moving funny?"

"I don't think so, why?"

Did the doctors not mention anything? "Have the doctor's said much about why you're in quarantine and what they might be looking for?"

"Not much. Just that I could've been exposed to a virus or something, and that it might take a couple weeks to know for sure."

Crap. "Well, the disease might affect a person's WHISP, too." Only a WHISP, but she doesn't need to worry about that.

"Oh."

"You haven't noticed anything strange with your own WHISP, have you?"

"No. I don't think so."

"Good, that's good."

She clears her throat. "Anything else?"

"No, but if you think of anything else you remember about that night, even if you don't think it's important, please don't hesitate to give me a call, okay?"

"Okay."

"Thank you for all your help, Isabel, and again, I'm so sorry about Yosef."

"Thank you, Detective."

Hanging up, I really hope that if there is some bioweapon in play, Isabel somehow avoided exposure.

CHAPTER 12

Excerpt from Transcript of Session 44:
Dr. Aziz Fritz with Det. S. Harbinger

Fritz: Do you think criminal WHISPers expect you to treat them leniently because you have a WHISP?
Harbinger: Oh yeah.
Fritz: That must be frustrating.
Harbinger: Yeah, but it happens a lot with women perps, too. We're both XX, can't you cut me some slack? I've dealt with it before.
Fritz: You don't find this any different?
Harbinger: I just try to treat people like people.
Fritz: But I'm sure you get accused of leniency.
Harbinger: Only about as often as I got accused of being too harsh, before.

AFTER MY INTERVIEW WITH ISABEL, I CHECK TO SEE IF the subpoena of names of residents of the shelter went through and finally get the list: Yosef Zimmerman, Isabel Winovich, Latrina Frank, Robert Schmidt, and Noi Donghae. Next, I look up the victims in the DMV database to give them faces, and get photos for all but Noi. She doesn't come up on a brief White Pages search of New York, either. She might be a recent immigrant, so I send off an email to the Department of Immigration. The shelter has only provided the names, no addresses or phone numbers, but I'm willing to bet they asked residents for at least an emergency contact, so I call them. The provided number goes straight to voice mail. Not surprising, if they're being harassed by the media. I leave a message asking for any other information on any of the victims and then have to wonder where all the wallets of the missing victims went. There are a lot of people I could ask, but I phone Crone.

"What do you want?" his voice is more jovial than cranky.

"Good afternoon to you, too."

"You know I'm just upstairs, right?"

"I'm sequestered down here right now." I grin. "And I know you aren't hauling your ass down into the basement."

"Touché."

"Why did we have to subpoena the names of the shelter victims? Weren't there IDs at the crime scene?"

"Only Yosef's."

"Don't you think that's odd?"

Crone hesitates. I picture him fiddling with one of his wide, ugly ties. "Maybe. But trying to hide the identity of a victim isn't weird. It's kinda common among criminals, really. Slows us down."

"Yeah, okay."

"So, how's my case going? I heard you got an arrest."

"Yeah, would you believe it's that asshole McCaffrey from CAW? Found his fingerprint in the van."

"Wow. He must be one huge fucking idiot. Like those husbands who 'find' the bodies of their spouses and are the first to call the police."

I chuckle. "Right." *Only...* "Only he didn't call the police right away."

"Couldn't have if he was in the van committing the crime."

"Right, but in order for it not to look suspicious, to make contacting the police with the video look like innocence, they would've called sooner. And why would they send the same guy who committed the crime to exonerate CAW? That doesn't make sense."

"Maybe to spit in our faces? Or give him a partial alibi? Wait, does he have an alibi?"

Letting out a huff, I sit back in my chair and glance at the clock: four thirty-two. "He hasn't mentioned one yet, but we're still waiting on his lawyer."

"Well, you know I like CAW for the kidnapping, in any case. Keep me posted, okay?"

"You joining the task force?"

"Nope."

"Then maybe I'll keep you posted."

I hang up as Green ambles over. "It's time."

"McCaffrey's lawyer finally show up?"

She nods. "Yep. Name's Lila something."

My eyebrows skyrocket up my forehead. "Lila Grant?"

"You know her?"

Oh crap. "Yeah. She gave me some unofficial information when I was working the Chester case."

"Ah. I can have Diwan do the interview instead, if you want."

"No. It's fine. It's just that she's good. If we have to go up against her in court, the case needs to be airtight, so we can't fuck up anything."

"Okay."

I get up to walk with her then hesitate. "Has the Chief already—"

"You're good to go."

"Great." Blood rushes from my stomach to my face as, once again, I'm reminded of the need for my isolation.

In silence, we head up the stairs and over to the interrogation room. Crone spots me and winks, and I respond with a slight nod. When we get closer, I see the Chief in the observation room and head in there first. Grant and McCaffrey are talking quietly. She's possibly wearing the exact same cleavage-baring outfit she wore when we first met and appears totally relaxed. McCaffrey, on the other hand, has a sheen of sweat on his forehead and bloodshot eyes. The Chief smiles at me when I enter.

"Chief, there's something you should know."

"Oh?" His smile slips.

"I have a history with Lila Grant."

"You do?"

"From the Chester copycat case." From the frown touching the corners of his mouth, I don't have to elaborate. He knows I met her after going a bit rogue. Meeting secretly with CAW was what got me thrown off the Chester copycat case.

"Is this going to be a problem?"

"Not at all." *Hopefully*.

He doesn't like it, but I stay quiet and he relents. "Fine."

Green's been waiting in front of the interrogation room door. I nod to her and we go in together.

Grant isn't surprised to see me. Smug maybe, but not surprised. She stands when we enter. "Detective Harbinger, I wish I could say it's nice to see you again." Her eyes drift to my WHISP then back to me.

Bitch. "Lila Grant, this is Detective Green. Detective Green, Lila Grant."

Green and Grant shake hands and size each other up before sitting.

As I take my seat, I glance at McCaffrey. He's either nervous because he got caught and Grant's pissed off she has to bail him out, or because he thinks CAW's going to throw him under the bus. I get the ball rolling. "Where was your client between the hours of 2 a.m. and 5 a.m. on the morning of Wednesday, February 12th?"

"I was—"

Grant shoots McCaffrey a did-I-give-you-permission-to-speak look. "He was at home asleep."

Green smirks. "Can anyone verify that?"

"You already know that my client lives alone in a building with no doorman, so you already know the answer is no."

"We don't want to make any assumptions." Green scribbles down the answer on a legal pad even though the interview's being recorded. Then she pulls out a photo of the van and slides it across the table. "Mr. McCaffrey, how did your fingerprint get onto the steering wheel of this van?"

Grant intercepts the photo and shakes her head. "My client has no idea, other than to say that he previously rented vehicles from that company, so maybe it somehow got transferred there."

What? "Transferred there?"

"Yes, Detective, transferred there accidentally, say from a sticky glove when an employee was cleaning multiple vehicles."

Keeping a neutral face, I glance sidelong at Green. Her face is a mask of incredulity. I'm about to call bullshit when Grant continues.

"But I'm not sure why that's relevant."

Okay, I'll bite. "You aren't sure why your client's fingerprint in a vehicle used to commit a crime is relevant?"

"Who says this vehicle was involved in a crime?"

We stare at each other and slowly it sinks in. Grant's seen the video. There's nothing distinguishing this white van from the white van in the video, but without a view of the license plate, there's also nothing to prove this is the van in the crime video either. The only thing that links it is the time frame it showed up on another camera, and the fact that it was stolen and appeared to be dumped, but that is all circumstantial. Trace must have found something other than the fingerprint in the van tying it to the crime, right?

"We have video evidence linking this van to the crime." Green is bluffing, but hopefully Grant doesn't notice.

"Oh, I assume that means you have a license plate match from the van parked in front of the shelter and the van you allegedly found my client's fingerprint in."

"Other evidence," Green evades.

"Oh, other evidence. Well, I'm sure it's evidence that will stand up to judicial scrutiny. Enough to hold my client, I'm sure."

This isn't going as planned. "We have additional evidence to link your client to the crime."

"I'm listening, Detective."

"Did you know, Mr. McCaffrey, that a number of the city's traffic cameras are out this week due to an upgrade in the system?"

McCaffrey looks to Grant and she shrugs.

"No. I didn't."

"You had no idea?"

"None."

Grant interjects. "Where is this going, Detective?"

"Did you know that the city's road commission records were hacked a few months ago?"

"No."

"Specifically, records involved in the city's traffic cameras and the upcoming shutdown associated with the upgrade?"

Grant holds up her hand. "No, Detective, my client had no idea about the hack. How could he?"

"Are you sure? Because the hack was traced back to an IP address at the CAW headquarters here in the city."

Now Grant is surprised. McCaffrey looks a little panicked, but his expression leans more toward, 'It wasn't me' than, 'Oh crap, I didn't cover my tracks.'

"We're in the process of obtaining a warrant for that computer. Unless CAW wants to just give it to us and save us the trouble."

Grant swallows and her face returns to cool and aloof. "CAW will be happy to turn over anything to the NYPD which we are required to by law, our previous generosity having gone unappreciated."

She better be talking about the videos in this case and not her previous help on the Chester case.

"Now, if you have no further questions for my client, I'd like you to release him based on lack of evidence."

"I'm sure you would." I stand. "We'll just need to organize some paperwork for that release."

Green collects the photo of the van, places it in her folder, and also stands. "Give us a few minutes, Counsel."

I head for the door.

"He's innocent, Detective."

Stunned by Grant's frankness, I turn.

"Whatever's going on here, CAW isn't involved, and your focus here is only hurting those people."

Is she serious right now? "I'm just following the evidence and CAW is where it's taking me."

"CAW is where they want it to take you."

"They who?"

"Who, indeed."

CHAPTER 13

Excerpt from Transcript of Session 29:
Dr. Aziz Fritz with Det. S. Harbinger

Fritz: You know I get paid whether you talk or not, right?
Harbinger: You're funny.
Fritz: Seriously, these sessions are much more effective when you
participate.
Harbinger: I don't feel like I have much to say today. Why don't
you ask me a question?
Fritz: Why don't you feel like you have much to say today?
Harbinger: [Makes lewd gesture.]

IN THE OBSERVATION ROOM, I STARE AT MCCAFFREY, trying to find someone who would treat a fellow human being like cattle. *Maybe.* Maybe, if he thought his actions could lead to a cure, but I still get the sense he'd ask for volunteers first and tranq dart them only as a last resort. Still, I can't ignore the evidence or CAW's history.

"Please tell me forensics found something else in that van to tie it to the kidnapping."

Green doesn't meet my eye.

"Are you fucking serious? Not even a thread from the stretcher sheets, a tear of plastic from the hazmat suits, a fiber of carpet from the shelter, nothing?"

She looks up. "I told you they wiped it clean."

"It's one thing to wipe something down, it's another thing to vacuum it, too." I pinch the bridge of my nose to ease a slow throb starting in my skull. "So, the only evidence we have to hold McCaffrey is the tech's trace of the city road commission to a CAW IP address."

"And that's a tenuous connection to the crime, at best."

"He's gonna walk. What about his apartment and CAW office?"

The Chief answers for Green, "Our teams haven't turned up anything damning yet at either location. There's evidence CAW was monitoring the city's WHISP shelters, but they also found CAW broke up a protest in front of a different shelter a month ago."

That tracks with what McCaffrey told me earlier. "Could they scrub that computer before the warrant for it comes through?"

"Probably not, but the judge added the computer on the warrant for McCaffrey's office, and tech is looking at it now."

Yes! "So, we hold him until they find something."

Shaking his head, the Chief sighs. "It's not enough." He points to Grant. "Your pal in there will argue that even if CAW knew about the traffic cam shut downs, that doesn't mean they perpetrated the kidnapping."

He's right. "Fine. I'll tell them." I yank the observation room door open, close it behind me, and take a deep, calming breath before opening the interrogation room door. Grant immediately stands.

"You and your client are free to go. There'll be some paperwork at the front desk. But as the investigation is still ongoing, I have to ask that you don't leave town."

She flashes me a shark-toothed smile. "Of course."

Grant gives me and my WHISP a wide berth as she leads McCaffrey from the room. She's back to smug, he's looking equal parts relieved and exhausted, with no trace of satisfaction. Right then, I know he's not the mastermind of all this, but it still doesn't mean he isn't CAW's fall guy, just in case. Regardless, he's not a real lead. I watch them walk away, then return to the observation room.

"Where are we on the second vehicle?"

———

After a painstaking tracking of all vehicles large enough to transport the kidnappers and victims headed south, we conclude they must've doubled back and start checking the other directions of travel. I was so sure they wouldn't bother. With the traffic cameras out, doubling back seemed like a waste of time, but the kidnappers were thorough —overly, stupidly thorough. Like someone who'd watched too many spy films thorough.

Confined to the basement again, my job is to double-check all the vehicles headed south that have already been cleared. There are eight: three vans and five trucks. Two of the vans have NY plates and one has a NJ plate.

All registered owners have already been called and have verified that they were driving past the cameras on Wednesday morning for legitimate reasons. I'm doing background checks for criminal records, CAW affiliations, recent financial problems, etcetera, and I'm not finding anything. Switching over to the trucks, my cell buzzes. It's past 7 p.m., so I'm expecting Ben, but it's Lincoln.

Lincoln: Hey Mom, how's it going?

Sylvia: I'm fine. How're you? Sorry you had to vacate your own apartment last night.

Lincoln: It's fine. I can stay with Naomi as long as I need to. Can you come into the lab tomorrow?

Sylvia: Not if you're there. Or any other WHISPer. I'm sure your dad told you.

Lincoln: He did. We'd clear it for you. Just want to take some measurements.

Sylvia: This sounds like WHISP human testing. Did you get approval? :P

Lincoln: This is serious, Mom.

Sylvia: I know. Okay. I'll talk to your dad tonight.

Lincoln: Thanks. Love you.

Sylvia: Love you too.

I put down the phone and stretch. Green's gone, the Chief's office is dark, and Brown and Clemont have come in for the night shift. It's probably time for me to head out. Tomorrow we'll interview family members of the victims, not that I think it'll matter much, in this case. There's nothing to indicate the kidnappers were after these specific victims, just WHISPers, but WHISPers who were easy targets. Additionally, if there was some kind of bioweapon test, they probably wanted to contaminate the shelter for other WHISPers. If we hadn't seen CAW's video, we would've never even suspected that. Which, if it was all true, made CAW's involvement and then handing over the video, make even less sense. *Hello square one, can I bang my head against you?* Yes, definitely time to go home.

———

BACK AT THE APARTMENT, BEN HAS MADE HIS SECOND go-to dinner. Grilled cheese sandwiches and Campbell's Tomato Soup. He's spooning soup into bowls when I reach the kitchen. A bouquet of roses in a crystal vase crowds the kitchen table. *What the—*

"Hey, Happy Valentine's Day." He sets down the ladle and

turns to give me a kiss. "How's the investigation going? I heard you had to release that CAW guy. That sucks."

Valentine's Day. Right. Totally wasn't on my radar. *Had we made plans?* "Maybe." I flop down into a chair. "Maybe not."

He sets a plate and a bowl in front of me. "Okay?"

"It was all circumstantial evidence and it doesn't really add up, anyway. I think he's a dead end."

"Oh." Ben sets his plate and bowl on the table and joins me. "Any new leads?"

I give him my what-do-you-think look.

"Right. If there were, you wouldn't be home eating dinner with me."

"Bingo." I take a bite of sandwich dipped in creamy, red goodness. This is way better than some fancy restaurant steak. My heart twinges with guilt. "Thanks for the roses. They're really pretty. I, uh, didn't get you anything. Sorry."

"It's fine, you've been busy." Ben moves his sandwich around on the plate but doesn't start eating. "You, ah, talk to Lincoln?"

I nod and swallow. "Said you two want me to go down to the lab tomorrow. What's that all about?"

"We just want to take some measurements of your WHISP particles."

Pausing mid-bite, I frown. "That's what he said, but doesn't that get dangerously close to testing, which, if I'm not mistaken, is still illegal?"

He still hasn't touched his sandwich. "Legallé nil legallé, is…grey area." His affected Russian accent is terrible.

"Okay. Two questions then. One, are you bending rules just because I'm your wife and, two, what are you hoping to find?"

"I hope we don't find anything, but if you were exposed to something that could affect your WHISP particles, maybe we can detect it and try to reverse it."

I notice he hasn't answered my first question, but let it go for now. "Wouldn't you rather test Isabel's WHISP? She's the one who was at ground zero."

"Love to, but she's still in quarantine for regular human diseases and we want to use some delicate equipment that we can't remove from the lab. And even if we could move them to her, hospitals have so much background radiation from their own equipment, the readings would probably be skewed."

I've dug into my dinner in earnest while he's talking, so I have to wipe soup from my chin before continuing. "But you'll have no baseline to compare to. You've never taken measurements of my WHISP before, so how will you know what's not normal?"

"Hey, look at you spouting scientific method at me."

I stick out my tongue, but something in his eyes makes me pull it back in and frown. "What?"

"We had to test the equipment."

The heavy weight of realization spreads over me. The task force didn't ask Lincoln to join because they thought he was some brilliant, budding particle physicist, they asked him because he's a budding particle physicist with a WHISP. He was their handy guinea pig this whole time, and he's not an idiot, so he probably knows it. Ben probably knew it, too, right from the beginning. "You let our son—"

"Sylvy, you know Lincoln, I never *let* him do anything. He made his own choice about this."

"But he's a fucking guinea pig."

"He wants to figure this thing out. He wants to help people. It's only a few measurements."

"For now. Christ, Ben, you know what messing with someone's WHISP can do."

"This is totally safe, I promise."

Head in my hands, I let out a long, slow breath. I do trust Ben, I do, yet there's a churning in my stomach. Maybe I'm mad at myself for not seeing all this earlier. It's not like I can ask Lincoln to quit the task force, and Ben's there to make sure he's safe. *This isn't CAW, Sylvy, this is the task force you yourself are on.*

"Sylvy?"

I look up. "Just don't…just don't let him do anything stupid."

"Like climbing into a particle accelerator?"

I bark out an angry laugh. "Cheap shot."

CHAPTER 14

Excerpt from Transcript of Session 51:
Dr. Aziz Fritz with Det. S. Harbinger

Fritz: Do you feel like we're making any progress?
Harbinger: Depends on what you mean by progress.
Fritz: Well, let's start with the original reason you started seeing
me, the nightmares. Are those any better now?
Harbinger: They're different, does that count?
Fritz: Are they still about WHISPs?
Harbinger: Technically, the first one wasn't about a WHISP.
Fritz: You know what I mean.

BEN'S NEW LAB IS PART OF THE BROADWAY COMPLEX and is two stories underground to help dampen stray electromagnetic radiation and shield it from radio waves. I've been here a few times before to visit Ben and Lincoln. It's not flashy. Cold, bare concrete hallways lead to one large lab and a few smaller ones with special equipment or isolated computers. We're in one of the smaller labs and I'm in a copper cage in the middle of the lab, sitting on a wooden stool whilst Ben fiddles with buttons and dials. He's pretty cute in his lab coat.

"Let me know if you start to feel anything."

I shift to relieve some of the pressure on my ass. "Like what?"

"If you start to feel dizzy, or light-headed, or sleepy—"

"Or dopey, or happy? Okay, I think I get it."

"Or if there's any pressure in your head or on your back."

I resist the urge to glance over my shoulder at Liv. *You behave now.* "I thought you said this was totally safe."

Ben turns back to the machine's glowing blue screen. "It is."

"Uh-huh."

"Just try to sit as still as possible."

"It'd be easier to sit still if this was a recliner instead of the world's most uncomfortable stool." *Ba-da-ching.*

"Sylvy, please." Ben recognizes my nervous humor.

"Why the cage, anyway?"

"It's a Faraday cage. It blocks out ambient electromagnetic fields so the equipment can focus solely on your WHISP's field."

Suddenly I'm claustrophobic. "So it's a WHISP cage. Like the one we talked about trapping Ray in."

Ben clears his throat. "Yeah. But it's fine as long as you don't move around too much."

I want to ask him how he knows that, but I close my eyes and think about the case instead of being in a cage having measurements taken that may cause pressure in my brain and might accidentally separate me from Liv and put me into a catatonic state. *Easy, right?*

Okay, I'm a terrorist group who hates WHISPs so much I've developed a WHISP virus or prion or something. I want to test it out on some WHISPers and see if it can continue to infect at a location, so I choose to hit a WHISP shelter with crappy security. I go through the trouble to hack into the city's road commission... Wait, why? How could I have known the city was updating the cameras and that some of them would be out? I...don't. I hack in to see where current cameras are so that I can avoid as many as possible. Pick my routes to and from the shelter.

"Sylvy."

"Hmmm."

"We're done."

I open my eyes. Ben has the cage door open. "Anything?" I ask.

He has his serious face on. "It'll take some time to compare your WHISP particle properties to Lincoln's."

I hop off the stool and rub my butt. "Seriously, get a more comfortable stool."

He hugs me as I exit the cage. "See, perfectly safe."

"I never doubted you, scientist man." *Well, not much.*

"Oooo, scientist man? I like the sound of that."

I force a smile. "Down, boy. I still have kidnap victims to find."

"Good luck."

"Thanks. I'll need it. We're talking to the families today."

———

WELL, THE REST OF THE TEAM IS TALKING TO families today. Because the victims were in a WHISP shelter, there's a high likelihood many of the family members have a problem with WHISPs, so I've been banished to the basement once more. With no new updates from tech, I restart my double-check of the possible second vehicles, but my brain is stuck back on the reconstruction I was doing in the cage. Then it hits me. We've been so focused on where the van was going after the attack, did anyone think to tell tech to check where the van had come from? I grab the phone and get Beaulieu.

"Beaulieu, it's Harbinger."

"We haven't found anything useful on any of the other surveillance videos you gave us, but there're months to go through."

"It's fine. I just wanted to ask you if anyone was checking where the van came from before it reached the shelter that night."

"Well, I didn't, but..." she covers the receiver and there's muffled talk punctuated by a muted expletive. "No. No one thought to do that. I'm on it now."

"Thanks. Keep me posted."

She hangs up. I don't take it personally.

———

LUNCH SOMEHOW COMES AND GOES AGAIN WITH ME none the wiser. It isn't until Crone shambles over to my desk with a greasy paper bag that I notice it's nearing 2 p.m.

"This area's restricted to task force members only."

He drops the bag on my desk. "Bullshit. You're welcome, by the way."

"What's this?"

He plants a butt cheek on the edge of my desk. "Burger from YahtzeeBurger."

I grab the bag. "Marry me."

"What do I get for the fries?"

I've already taken a huge bite of the burger, so I can't reply right away. When I can breathe again, I smirk. "You lose points for forgetting a Coke."

He reaches into his jacket pocket and produces a red can.

"Damn, Crone. I... Wait, what's going on?"

He rubs the stubble on his chin. "I take it you haven't seen the news this morning."

"No, I had…a doctor's appointment this morning."

"Uh-huh. Well, then you missed quite the story."

The second bite of burger catches in my throat. With difficulty, I swallow it down. "What story?"

"The one about your sabotage of the kidnapping investigation leading to the release of the CAW suspect."

"Ah." Angry isn't the right word. I've been angry before and it didn't include boiling organs.

"So how is the investigation going?"

I don't bother explaining to Crone that all the evidence against McCaffrey was circumstantial. I'm sure he's already heard all about it. "CAW doesn't make sense because it makes too much sense."

"That makes no sense."

"I don't think whoever did this expected them to be monitoring the shelters like they were. Or that they would come forward to the police with the video."

"Unless it's all a confusing smoke screen."

I polish off some fries. "That's just too long a con for my tastes. And what if we'd done some tech wizardry and gotten the license plate from some reflection from the original video? Nah, too risky."

He shrugs. "What are you working on right now?"

"I'm double-checking possible second vehicles, but these have already been cleared once. We think the other vehicle doubled back, so now we're having to check vans and trucks in every direction and that means requesting footage from a bunch more private cameras since about half the traffic cameras were out that night. So, pretty much running around in circles, but tech is also trying to pinpoint where the van came from, so maybe that'll be easier."

Crone grunts and heaves himself up. "Well, you have fun with that."

After cramming more fries into my mouth, I scoff, "Thanks.

But really, thanks for the lunch. How'd you know I hadn't already eaten?"

"Because you're you."

Good point. He ambles toward the elevator and I return to my computer screen. The last truck's license plate is registered to a shipping company in New Jersey, Radcliffe Imports, Inc. We'd already called and confirmed a shipment of Chinese imports from New York early Wednesday morning, but I'm calling again to get the name of the driver, so I can clear them, as well. I punch the number in and lean back in my chair when my ear is assaulted by the jarring three tones of a disconnected number. Huh, must've misdialed. Rechecking the number, I dial again with the same result. Tingles run through my arms down to my fingers as I hang up and try to bring up the company's website. All I get is a message saying the website is down for routine maintenance. Alarm bells are ringing in my head now, but there's one more thing to check before getting everyone's hopes up.

I ring the dock the truck was supposed to have picked up its shipment from and ask for the dock master. My heart racing, each second I'm on hold takes roughly an hour. "Come on."

"Hello?"

"Hello. My name is Detective Harbinger. I'm with NYPD. I need some information on a shipment from your dock early Wednesday morning. The shipment was from China and was received by a company called Radcliffe Imports, Inc. from New Jersey."

"All right. Let me get in the records." A pause. "You say it was from Wednesday morning? This Wednesday?"

"Yes, Wednesday, February 12th."

"Hmmm."

Already, I have a pretty good idea of what he's going to say. "What is it?"

"Well, Detective, we didn't have any Chinese vessels in

dock on Wednesday morning, and I can't see that we've ever had a shipment from a Radcliffe Imports."

"You're sure? R-a-d-c-l-i-f-f-e."

"I'm sure."

Holy shit. "Thank you."

Excerpt from Transcript of Session 37:
Dr. Aziz Fritz with Det. S. Harbinger

Fritz: Can we talk about your parents?
Harbinger: What about them? I don't want to talk about the
murder anymore. We've been over it.
Fritz: Were they tolerant people?
Harbinger: What?
Fritz: How would they have felt about the WHISP phenomenon?
Harbinger: I don't know. I didn't really get a chance to know
them that well.
Fritz: You must've heard stories about them from family
members, gotten an impression of them, their views.
Harbinger: Not really. Everyone only says nice things to you
about your parents when they're horribly murdered.

IT'S ONLY BY PROMISING TO STAY IN THE CAR THE entire time that the Chief allows me to accompany Green and Diwan to the address we got off the Radcliffe Imports website before it shut down. In the manufacturing district of Bayonne, NJ, we drive past the address on New Hook Road and find a warehouse with a new banner tied to the fence entitling the property Radcliffe Imports, Inc. The gate's locked with a rusty padlock and from the looks of the building beyond, the only activity the place has seen in years is someone putting up the banner, but looks can be deceiving. We meet up with local officers behind the shipping office of the oil company down the road. Since none of them have WHISPs, Green rolls down the window and motions the four of them over.

"Officer Froesch?"

The older man with mahogany skin nods and removes his sunglasses. "You must be Detective Green."

Green nods and motions to me. "And this is Detective—"

When Froesch spots me in the passenger's seat he scowls. "Harbinger."

He must watch the news. I nod as his eyes wander to the backseat.

Green ignores the tension. "So, any activity?"

He returns his attention to her. "It's hard to get eyes on the front gate, there's no cover, but we have a plain clothes deputy watching the back of the warehouse from another of the oil company's buildings. He hasn't seen anything, and I talked to some of the oil company employees. None of them remember seeing any activity in the past few weeks except the sign going up."

Damn.

"Any idea who owned it before?"

"Nah. The foreman here said it's been vacant for a year or more. Before that, it was also some kind of import business warehouse, but they did have trucks coming in and out."

Green turns to me. "What do you think?"

I shake my head. "Looks like a dead end, but I'd hate to be wrong."

She nods. "Same." Then turns to Froesch. "If you were going to take the warehouse, what would your plan be?"

Leaning on the car, he licks his lips. "You think there're hostages in there?"

"Maybe."

"I'd wait till dark, cut access holes through the fence, get as close as we can, and then bust through with SWAT maybe."

I touch Green's shoulder. "The shelter was cleared for all the usual bioweapons, right? No need for suits?"

"Did she say bioweapons?"

Green sighs. "The kidnappers wore hazmat suits, but the original scene's been cleared by the New York Health Department for all known dangerous biologicals."

Froesch pulls an uncertain frown.

"I'm sure your SWAT team has masks for this sort of thing. But they can't have any WHISPers on the team. We haven't cleared something designed for them specifically."

His face twists. "Not to worry. But doesn't your fancy task force have a team for this?"

WHISP bigot. Figures.

"We could get NYPD SWAT in here if Jersey isn't up for this."

Froesch spits. "I didn't say that."

"Well, then let's get the wheels turning."

———

"I CAN'T BELIEVE YOU'RE NOT GOING IN," I SAY.

Green takes a sip of her fast food cola and shrugs. "It's not like SWAT needs or wants me under their heels. We'll have their video feed and if there's something there, we're less than a minute down the road. Have you ever gone in with SWAT before?"

Not for a long while. Guess I'm just feeling left out. "A long time ago."

"Right. Plus, you don't think the victims are in there,

anyway. This way, you don't accidentally get shot by an over-amped ball of testosterone."

"I understand Newark has at least three women on the SWAT team now."

"Good for them."

The police radio in Green's car crackles to life, its green receiving light glowing in the car's dim interior. "All units are in place. Awaiting go signal."

I adjust the laptop on my lap. The screen is dark, but the SWAT team haven't turned on their infrared goggles and cameras yet and the warehouse only has one weak exterior light near the front gate. No interior lights that we could see have come on in the building since nightfall.

Green picks up the receiver. "Officer Froesch, is your team a go?"

The local Bayonette police are all in monitoring positions around the warehouse and several blocks away to alert us of approaching vehicles.

"Bayonette unit is a go."

Green looks to me and I nod.

"NYPD is a go."

"SWAT, we are in the green. Ready. And. Go, go, go!"

Suddenly my screen comes to life with grainy, green images. Green and I watch as a SWAT member wearing goggles and a bulky mask cuts through the fence with heavy duty wire cutters and quickly pulls back the fencing so other team members can run through the hole. Our SWAT cameraman is the second one through and in minutes the whole unit is at the windowless, concrete wall of the warehouse. Slower now, they make their way along the building's perimeter and then round the corner and stop. This side of the building has a door. Only the lead team member approaches the door and then tries the knob. Unsurprisingly, it's locked. The radio crackles softly.

"Team Beta in place at west door."

His announcement is followed closely by several other confirmations of placement and readiness. My chest tightening, I glance up at Green. "Here we go."

"You are go for entry, SWAT. Ready. And. Go, go, go!"

We watch the first SWAT figure hoist a ramming bar and bash it into the side door: once, twice. On the third impact, the door crashes open, nearly coming off its hinges. The rammer now stands clear and our SWAT person is the first to enter the building. As the dust settles, light appears across a vast, empty interior. It's another team breaking through the front door.

My heart drops. Nothing. "Damn."

———

It took a few hours to completely clear the building and grounds and I had to violate my promise to the Chief not to leave the car several times, but made sure no one was in the oil company building when I went in to pee. By the time the NYPD forensics team arrived, the layer of dust on the floor of the warehouse pretty much told the story. The warehouse was a sham. No one had been inside this building in months. Our only hope for evidence was from the Radcliffe Imports, Inc. banner, which was carefully cut down and collected. They also dusted the fence, lock on the gate, and doorknobs inside and out for fingerprints, but came up empty.

By the time Green and I return to the precinct, it's after eleven. I'd texted Ben some of the details of where I was and about how long I thought I'd be there. He was pretty pissed off. I couldn't blame him too much. I'd been of absolutely zero assistance, my legs were cramped from sitting in a car all afternoon and all evening, and I could've accidentally exposed another WHISPer to my potentially infected WHISP. Still, I was glad I'd been there. It made me feel more a part of the case, even if it hadn't turned up anything terribly useful.

I barely sit down at my desk when Clemont comes over.

"How'd it go?"

He's already heard the basics, so I skip to details. "We might get something off the banner. Any luck tracking the building's ownership?"

He nods. "But you're not going to like it."

"Why not?"

"It doesn't belong to anyone."

"How does that work?"

Clemont shrugs. "Went into foreclosure for back-taxes or something and then the credit union folded and it got lost in the paperwork shuffle."

"And Radcliffe Imports, Inc.?"

"Never an actual company. Website address was routed through Taiwan and couldn't be traced after that."

Shit on a stick. "How long was the site up for?"

"Only a couple of months."

Don't break things, stay calm. "Where are we on tracking where the white van came from before it arrived at the shelter?"

"Still working on it. That area has a lot fewer private cameras with views of the street."

"Right."

"You going home?"

I look from Clemont to the room to my dark computer, feel the weight of my eyelids, and compare it to the weight of my heart. "Do you need me?"

"Not at all."

The failure of the day is really sinking in now. "Then I guess I'll see you tomorrow."

CHAPTER 16

Excerpt from Transcript of Session 33:
Dr. Aziz Fritz with Det. S. Harbinger

Fritz: Are you ready to talk about Chester?
Harbinger: She was…was a murderer.
Fritz: She isn't a murderer anymore?
*Harbinger: She isn't anything anymore. Losing her WHISP
broke her.*
Fritz: You've previously described her as "broken."
Harbinger: Not like this.
Fritz: So, this break absolves her of her former murders?
*Harbinger: We can't know who was in control when the murders
happened.*
*Fritz: So, you think she wasn't in control of her WHISP when it
murdered those people.*
Harbinger: I didn't say that.

WITH THE NEW DAY CAME…NOTHING. RADCLIFFE
Import, Inc. was still a dead end, though we continued trying to
trace the truck's route out of the city. Ben was still pouring

over the data he'd collected from my WHISP, I was still on partial duty, tech still hadn't been able to trace where the white van had come from, and we still had no further evidence linking Rondell McCaffrey and CAW to the crime. I was starting to miss a good old-fashioned murder. Though murder was still part of this, I'd almost completely forgotten about it. I call Claire at the medical examiner's office.

She answers on the second ring. "I was wondering when you'd get back around to me."

I smile, but it doesn't last long. "Um, how did your quarantine go?"

"Wonderful. Nothing like being in quarantine *and* having the body you're working on in quarantine. I was trying to do an autopsy in a suit on a body in bubble surrounded by another bubble. Also, so fun being quarantined with a bunch of dead bodies."

"Oh come on, you love it down there."

She laughs. "Yeah, but it's not very comfortable."

"Did someone order you pizza?"

"No. I had a leftover sandwich. You got pizza!"

Whoops. "It wasn't very good pizza."

"Just stop talking." I can hear the smile in her voice. "What did you want, anyway?"

"Did you find anything unusual with Yosef? Anything helpful?"

"He had a brain tumor, does that help?"

Huh. "Maybe, actually. The witness said he was able to do unusual things with his WHISP. Do you think the tumor could have had something to do with that?"

"Hmmm. Well, oligodendrogliomas have a myelin sheath and facilitate nerve impulses, so I suppose one could maybe amplify the electrical impulses in the brain, and it's thought that those impulses have an effect on WHISP particles, sooo maybe? But Chester didn't, sorry, doesn't have a tumor, right?"

A wave of nausea crests then settles. I swallow. "No, but the brains of psychopaths are different than normal brains too, right?"

"That's true."

"Something to discuss with Ben, I guess. Anything else? I don't suppose there was any trace evidence that was missed? And ballistics has the bullet, right?"

"Let's see, I didn't note any other signs of illness or disease other than some emphysema, no trace for you, and I think they've got the bullet, but it had to be sterilized, so it might've taken a bit longer to get to them."

"Well, you can't break a case for me every time." I'm not expecting much from ballistics, but I should probably see if they found anything.

"Sorry to disappoint."

"Don't worry about it. We need to do dinner soon."

"I'll pencil you in for when this case is over."

It's already feeling cold to me, but I admire Claire's optimism. "Sounds good."

———

"Yep, it's a .40 caliber bullet."

I rest my head on my hand and scratch at a groove in the surface of my desk. "Anything unique?"

"Well, lands and grooves say it was fired from a Glock 22, but unless you have a suspect weapon, I'm not sure what else I can tell you."

"I don't suppose it matches anything in the database?"

"Sorry."

Ballistics is a bust, as predicted. "Thanks, Hess."

"No problem."

"Wait, one more thing. Do you need a permit to buy a tranquilizer gun?"

"Um, a tranquilizer gun?"

Am I really this out of leads? "Yeah, you know, the ones that shoot darts instead of bullets."

"I don't think you need a permit to buy the gun or the darts. The problem would be buying the tranquilizer to fill the darts with and that's not my department. You probably want to hit up Danny Won over in narco for that."

"Okay, will do. Thanks, Hess."

"No problem."

So, what am I thinking here? Tracking down tranquilizer gun purchases? I do a little internet digging and find out you can buy the guns at ranch supply stores, no questions asked. I don't even bother calling Danny. I know from previous cases that veterinary clinics are a great place to steal things like tranquilizers and drugs like Special K. *Argh. Think, Sylvy, think. What are you missing? Besides four people.*

I resist the urge to call Beaulieu. She might actually murder me for interrupting her work. I get up and wander over to Green's desk. It looks like she's filling out paperwork on the SWAT action at Radcliffe Imports.

"So, I meant to ask about the family interviews. Anything there?"

Green looks up. "Well, there are a few family members who are pretty happy the abduction happened, but other than that, just grieving, angry people."

"Seriously, there were relatives who were happy?"

She nods. "A brother who was glad he wouldn't have to deal with his freak sister anymore was the standout."

"That'd be Latrina's brother?"

"Uh-huh."

"Could you track down any of Noi's relatives?"

A heavy sigh. "We're still looking. We do know she immigrated about a year ago from South Korea, and that she had a WHISP when she immigrated."

"That's it?"

"She'd been at the shelter for three months, didn't give an emergency contact, and she didn't have a driver's license, so no address on file."

"Didn't she need to have an address of where she was staying when she came over?"

Green nods. "She did. It was a YWCA and no one there remembered her."

Guilt gnaws at me. We could do more digging. Many hotels hire recent immigrants in housekeeping and as kitchen staff, but in this case, since she wasn't the specific target of the crime, it wouldn't get us any closer to finding her. Still, what else am I going to do today? "I take it trace didn't find anything like a fingerprint on the banner?"

"Not that I've heard."

"The oil company have any surveillance cameras that might've caught who put up the banner?"

"Nope." She gives me a can-I-finish-my-paperwork-now look.

Again, I'm a little jealous of her paperwork. That's just wrong. "Right, well, I'll leave you to it, then."

As I head back to my desk, my mind centers on the banner. It wouldn't be something you could make at home. It had to have been ordered, then delivered somewhere. I Google banners and with some search tweaks, hit a few possible source companies. I'm halfway through dialing the first number when Ben calls. It's still well before lunch, so the little hairs on the back of my neck stand up.

"Ben, what is it?"

Brief silence, then, "Sylvy, we've found some…irregularities. Lincoln and I want you to come back to the lab for some more measurements."

Heart racing, instinctively I glance back at Liv who glances back at nothing. She…it seems fine. I feel fine, no dizziness, no mental fog, and not even a migraine. Though now with my skyrocketing pulse, I do feel slightly light-headed. *Deep, slow breath.*

"Sylvy?"

"Are you sure? I feel fine, and I'm actually working on something right now. Can it wait until tomorrow?"

"I'd rather not."

An itch tickles the back of my throat. "What kind of irregularities?"

Ben sighs through the receiver. "Differences in the behavior of your WHISP particles and standard WHISP particles."

"And by standard, you mean Lincoln's."

"Yes."

"Well, everyone's WHISP particles probably act a little different, right?" *Hmmm, am I in denial?*

"Probably, but if we measure yours again today, we can see if the differences are greater and compare the measurements to yesterday's measurements."

"But there could also be day to day variations, right?" *Yep, denial.*

"We measured Lincoln's particles for a month straight and saw less than one percent variation."

They tested Lincoln for an entire month. My baby, the guinea pig. The shock of Ben's statement quickly fades. What did I think when he'd told me they tested the equipment on Lincoln, that they'd done it once?

"Sylvy?" his voice is softer now.

I don't know if it's wholly the denial, or being right in the middle of contacting the banner manufacturers, or my being pissed at Ben for using our son in the lab, but I dig in my heels.

"I'm fine. I'm right in the middle of something here. I'll go in tomorrow morning."

"How about tonight?" He rushes to add, "If nothing else comes up with the case?"

Deep breath. In through the nose, out through the mouth. "Fine. I'll text you when I leave the precinct."

"Okay. I love you."

"I know...I love you, too."

CHAPTER 17

Excerpt from Transcript of Session 57:
Dr. Aziz Fritz with Det. S. Harbinger

Fritz: Do you still wish you'd been able to get away to that cabin in Montana?
Harbinger: That's not the way things worked out.
Fritz: If things had gone differently. Say, if there had been a simple copycat.
Harbinger: You're asking me if I would give up my relationship with Lincoln to not have a WHISP.
Fritz: Okay. Would you?
Harbinger: It's a stupid question.
Fritz: Why?
Harbinger: Because…because I can't change what happened.

AFTER ANOTHER LUNCH OF DUMPLINGS—MAN DO I love me some dumplings—and another brief chat with Green, I'm calling the fifth banner company when it occurs to me that it could've been a local job, too. I'm jotting down a note to check local NJ copy centers when someone finally answers.

"Banner-a-rama, how can I help you?"

"Hi there, my name is Detective Sylvia Harbinger and I'm with NYPD. We're trying to track the purchase of a banner for a company we're investigating."

"Oh. Okay. Um. What's the name of the company?"

"Radcliffe Imports, Inc. That's what the banner said, as well. It was a twenty-five foot banner and the address was in Bayonette, New Jersey."

"Radcliffe?"

"Yeah, Radcliffe Imports, Inc. R-a-d-c-l-i-f-f-e." A yawn blossoms. I turn my head and cover the receiver then take a sip from my lunch Coke.

"Right. Can I put you on hold?"

"Sure."

Light jazz comes on and I doodle a stick figure with a WHISP on my notepad. A few minutes pass before there's a click and the music dies. At first, I think I've been disconnected, but then a distinctly male voice, not the woman I'd previously spoken to, comes on. This is an older, much more authoritative voice.

"I'm sorry, Ma'am, but our purchase history is private. Is there anything else I can help you with today? We're running a special this week on fifteen-foot banners for ten percent off."

That gets my dander up. I straighten in my chair. "Hello, this is *Detective* Harbinger with the New York Police Department. I'm calling in regards to a kidnapping case and I need some information about a banner that might've been purchased from your company."

He clears his throat. "I'm sorry, Detective, but I'm going to need some kind of verification that you are who you say you are. Perhaps you could mail us a formal request on official police letterhead?"

Perhaps I could arrest you for obstruction of justice, asshole. "I will be happy to email you a request"—I start typing an official email—"but as I mentioned, this is a kidnapping case and very time sensitive, so your timely cooperation is greatly appreciated." *Bam.* I hit send. "You should be receiving the email any moment now." *But seriously, how many fake police requests could you possibly get?*

"Oh. Well, let me check my email." A pause. "I'm sorry, but I don't…oh, yes, there it is." Another pause. "Well, it may take us a little time to check our records and I'll want to call your supervisor just to make sure. Privacy policies. You understand."

I don't understand why this dickface is making things so difficult. I want to tell him that none of his competitors had any trouble with my fucking credentials. At this point, I'm about ninety-nine percent sure he did fill this order and is trying to cover his ass so he doesn't get in trouble somehow.

"I'm not sure I do understand, since this is such a simple request, but you can contact Chief Lowman at 212-555-2726, extension 044. I'll tell him to expect your call within the hour, and as soon as you have that information for me, you can either call me at the same number, ext. 047 or email me. Again, that number is 212-555-2726, extension 044. The number should also be on the request I emailed you."

"Right, fine, okay, but—"

I've been navigating Banner-a-rama's website. "Your corporate office is located in Tulsa, Oklahoma. Is that correct?"

"Yes."

"Great. Thank you for your cooperation, Mr.?"

He clears his throat. "Damon Grovener."

"And how do you spell that?"

"G-r-o-v-e-n-e-r."

"Perfect. And you're part of the company in what capacity?" It's taking a little time to put some fear of retribution into him, but I don't want any more feet-dragging on his part.

"Assistant Director of Sales and Marketing."

"Got it. Thank you, Mr. Grovener, I'll look forward to your prompt reply, as will Chief Lowman."

"Right."

"Goodbye."

He still sounded way too cocky. I really wish that slapping him with obstruction of justice wouldn't seriously impede the case. Glancing up, it doesn't look like the Chief's in his office, so I shoot him a text.

Harbinger: Was following up Radcliffe Imports banner. Probably purchased from online company called Banner-a-rama, but assistant director there pig. Expect his call within the hour to "verify" my badge.

Reluctantly, I replace "pig" with "unhelpful."

————

It's over three hours later when Grovener finally phones the Chief, probably in the hopes that he's left for the day, and with many insincere apologies for how slow their computer system is and how difficult it is for them to track orders sometimes, he finally emails me the purchase information about a half-hour after that. I've been busying myself with calling hotels in the area of the shelter to try to track down Noi's possible employer, but spinning my wheels, so my heart skips a beat when his email pops up in my in-box. My finger hovers over the mousepad. *Don't get too excited, this is probably another dead end.* I click it open.

The banner was purchased by Radcliffe Imports, Inc., so no surprises there. The phone number and email address are the same defunct ones from the taken-down website, and the street address is for the warehouse in Bayonette, NJ. A note for the delivery tells the company to leave the package at the gate. *Damn.* I move on to the payment information and find a credit card issued to the company president, you have got to be fucking kidding me, John D Smith. My heart sinks, but I call the credit card company anyway. With much less questioning of my authority than Banner-a-rama, they confirm the issue of the company card to Mr. Smith only a month ago.

"So, what you're saying is we shouldn't expect payment of the coming credit card statement?"

Ha. She's quite glib for a customer service agent. "Probably not, but don't cancel the card, and let us know if there's any more activity on it."

"Of course. But they're very close to their $1500 limit, so my guess is they won't try to use it again."

Damn. "Can you email me a copy of the statement?"

"No problem. There are some other charges on it."

Other charges? "Oh?"

"Yeah, there's a charge from Guns Unlimited for $865.97 and a charge for $406.56 from CompUServer Plus."

Guns Unlimited is probably the tranquilizer guns, but what the hell's the other charge for? "CompUServer Plus?"

"Yep. $406.56."

"Okay. Thanks for all your help."

"I'll email you that statement right away, Detective. Good luck with your case."

"Thank you." *Now why can't everyone be like her?*

———

"HELLO, COMPUSERVER CUSTOMER SERVICE LINE, this is Anthony, how can I help you?"

With the broken English and background noise, I'm doubting his name is really Anthony. "Hello, Anthony, my name is Detective Sylvia Harbinger and I'm with the New York Police Department. We're investigating a case your company may be able to help us with."

"Okay. Let me transfer you to our special orders division. One moment."

"No, wait! Hello?"

Soft pop music comes on. *Crap.* I groan. Wait, why would he think a police detective wanted to place an order for something? While on hold, I take a closer look at the CompUServer Plus website. It looks like they mainly work on setting up company computer systems and servers, but then at the bottom I spot the special orders button. It takes me a moment to process the new page that comes up. It appears CompUServer Plus also produces IP address modifying and tracing software for law enforcement and criminals alike.

"Special orders, this is Tina, how can I assist you?"

This connection is much less noisy. "Hi, Tina, this is Detective Sylvia Harbinger with the New York Police Department. I'm actually calling for some information on a purchase made a few weeks ago."

"Of course. A purchase from the NYPD?"

"Ah, no, actually, a purchase made by a private company called Radcliffe Imports, Inc. It was for $406.56 and was made on January 29th."

"May I ask why the NYPD is interested in the purchase?"

Oh, please don't make me prove my fucking credentials again, woman. "It's part of an active kidnapping investigation."

"Oh dear. You said Radcliffe Imports was the customer?"

"Yes. R-a—"

"Here it is. They purchased a software package for modifying and rerouting IP addresses."

My left eyebrow goes up. "That's legal?"

"Of course. Many of our clients are worried about their internet security and IP modification and rerouting is one of the many ways to protect a mainframe from hacking."

"Uh-huh. It also allows criminals to hide illegal internet activity."

"Unfortunately. However, if this is part of a criminal investigation, CompUServer Plus would be happy to look at any confiscated servers or hard drives to determine if and how our software was used."

If only we had...wait. "Would you be able to trace your software back from a computer, as well?"

"I'm not sure what you mean."

"If the software directed a signal through a specific IP address of a specific computer, say, to make it look as if a hacking attempt was coming from a specific computer, could your company trace back its software to the original computer?"

"Ah. Hmmm. I think so. Our programmers often fold in ways to distinguish our code from other companies' code, so we may be able to trace it back. If you could send us the hard drive of the computer in question, I can see what might be possible."

Sounds like a long process, if I can even get tech to agree to an outside consultation. "I don't suppose you have an office in New York."

"Of course. One of our main offices is on 54th street."

"Would your programmers be willing to work with NYPD forensic technology personnel?"

Tina's voice sharpens with excitement. "I think so. Your personnel might have to sign a non-disclosure agreement for access to some of our proprietary code, but yes, I think so."

"Brilliant."

————

It's nearing 5 p.m. when I get a call.

"Harbinger."

"It's Beaulieu. You were right. The hacking link to McCaffrey's computer was bogus. Directed through his computer by CompUServer Plus's software."

He really was framed. "By whom?"

A huff comes through the line. "Learning that's going to be a little trickier, apparently."

"But not impossible?"

"Not impossible, just not going to happen tonight, probably."

Crap. "When do you think?"

"Hard to say, but they're working their butts off over here."

"Nice to have such full cooperation."

Beaulieu laughs. "Well, it's not entirely altruistic. They've been selling the department pretty hard on some of their new tracing software."

"Sounds like they already have some police customers."

"Oh yeah, my buddy over at San Antonio PD swears by their products, but they're pretty pricey. Budgeting would really have to take a good long look at the percentage of cases projected to be solved and how many of those cases we actually get a year."

"I'll just be happy if we get somewhere with this case."

"Hey, at least we know it won't take us back to that fucking warehouse in Jersey again."

I chuckle. "Thank God."

"It didn't even have an internet connection."

CHAPTER 18

Excerpt from Transcript of Session 27:
Dr. Aziz Fritz with Det. S. Harbinger

Fritz: So, you haven't been going to the group sessions.
Harbinger: I went to one. I've been busy: PT, apartment hunting,
paperwork for the new task force... There's been a lot to do.
Fritz: Okay. So tell me about the one session you went to.
Harbinger: It was fine.
Fritz: Fine? Does that mean you found it helpful?
Harbinger: Honestly? Not really.
Fritz: Why do you think that is?
Harbinger: I don't know. I just didn't...connect with anyone
there.
Fritz: And that lack of connection didn't have anything to do
with the density of WHISPs in the room?
Harbinger: Is that why you recommended it?
Fritz: Exposure therapy is one of the most effective forms of
phobia treatment.
Harbinger: You're a bastard.

AROUND 6 P.M., HAVING CONFIRMED WITH GUNS

Unlimited that they delivered the tranquilizer guns to the Radcliffe Imports warehouse, I'm deep into trying to track the time and date of delivery of both the banner and the tranquilizer guns and coordinate that with traffic camera footage of someone picking up the guns and putting up the sign. I've been on hold with the logistics company used by Banner-a-rama for approximately twenty minutes when my cell buzzes. It's Ben.

Ben: New lead?

Me: How'd you know?

Ben: You were supposed to text.

I'd completely forgotten about promising Ben I'd go back into the lab tonight if nothing came up.

Me: Oh right. Yes. New lead.

Ben: Do they need you?

Heat flares in my cheeks.

Me: What's that supposed to

I delete it. Glancing up, I see Green's vacated desk. Clemont is sipping coffee and staring at his computer screen. No. They don't need me. I can hand this off to Clemont. I should. My butt's numb from sitting at my desk and I haven't even thought about dinner.

Me: No. But I'm hungry. If I meet you at lab, I might get hangry. Angry emoji.

Ben: What if I promise food waiting at lab?

Me: That's blackmail.

Ben: Smiley face with halo emoji.

BEN AND A PIZZA ARE WAITING FOR ME IN THE LOBBY when I arrive. He looks like shit. Dark circles hang on the bags under his eyes, his clothes are rumpled, and his hair has the greasy faux-hawk it gets when he runs his fingers through it too much, but he smiles salaciously and opens the cardboard box when I approach.

"Aaaah, see? It's your favorite."

He's gone all out. It is my favorite. A Sicilian-style flavor profile from Napoleon's Pie with thin lemon slices, garlic, and sea salt. My mouth waters, but he snaps the box shut and, still grinning, takes a few steps toward the elevator with it. His silliness is both endearing and frightening.

"You're funny."

"I try." His grin slips. "Shall we?"

I follow him into the elevator and a floor passes in silence as the scent of the pizza fills the space.

"So, tell me about this new lead."

Where to start? "Well, remember how we tracked the hack of city files to McCaffrey's computer at CAW?"

"Yeah."

"Well, turns out some other company routed the hack through his computer."

"No shit, really?"

I nod. "Yeah, it really is starting to look like someone is trying to frame CAW for this."

"Wow. That's huge. Any idea who?"

Simultaneously, the elevator doors open, my stomach growls loudly, and I fail to stifle a massive yawn. "Nah-ah-ah-aught, yet."

Ben heads to the main lab door and tries to juggle unlocking it and holding the pizza until I take the box from him.

"Isn't the cage in the other room?"

He finally gets the door unlocked and props it open so I can walk in ahead of him. "Yeah, but let's eat first."

The lab only has a few lights lit until Ben flicks a switch on the wall.

I set the pizza on Ben's desk, plop down in his chair, open

the box, and pull out a slice, trying to eat it over the box. "You guys don't have a night shift?"

Ben grabs some paper towels from a dispenser and hands me a couple. "Not officially, no. I mean, we aren't doing anything ground-breaking, at the moment. Maybe once we are in an actual testing phase instead of just models."

A shudder runs up my spine, pulling my shoulder blades together. I want to believe Ben means animal testing, but I don't think he does. The pizza slice I've just inhaled threatens to make a second appearance. I lean back and wipe my mouth. "Do you have a Coke?"

His chewing pauses and Ben shifts his weight before swallowing. "Can I get you some water instead? Caffeine might affect the measurements."

Ugh. "Fine. But I want a Coke after we're done...and a lollipop."

He winks at me and rinses out his coffee mug in a lab sink before filling it with water and handing it over.

I inspect the water, then look up at him. "You sure that's safe?"

"I drink it."

"That explains a lot." I sip the water and take a deep breath to keep the pizza down.

"You still feeling okay?"

"I'm fine."

He sets his pizza down in the lid of the box. "You're not inhaling your favorite pizza. Something's wrong."

I take another sip then select a second piece. "Give me a minute. I'm trying to pace myself." Studying the lemon slices, a pang of pain shoots through my heart. Lincoln hates lemon on pizza, says it's just wrong. "How's Lincoln?"

"He's fine. Worried about you, of course."

A thought strikes me. "Ben, what if I'm always contagious." *What if I can never hug Lincoln again?*

He shakes his head. "That's not...we don't even...let's not worry about that now. Let's just get these measurements and go from there." He picks up his pizza again and takes a bite.

I set mine down. "Does it look weird? I mean, different."

His eyes find mine then skip over my shoulder. "No. I don't think so."

I get up and wave my arms around. "What about now?"

He chucks his pizza back into the box and grabs my arms. "Sylvy, stop." He pulls me into a hug.

My eyes sting and I blink and sniff back tears. "Let's just do the measurements."

"Okay."

We head down the hall and once more Ben shuts me up in the copper cage. The stool is even more uncomfortable this time around and I'm unable to distract myself with the case because all I can picture is me waving at Lincoln through a plexiglass barrier, though watching Ben futz with the equipment through the copper wires isn't much more comforting. Also, this time I swear I do feel some pressure against my eardrums and picture Liv bringing her hands up to her ear silhouettes. Time slows to a crawl and an itch pricks up between my shoulder blades. Yet, I almost feel like I've been dozing when Ben opens the cage door.

"All done."

———

AFTERWARDS, NOT EVEN THE COKE BEN RETRIEVES from the vending machine cheers me as we drive home together, and once home I retreat to the bedroom. After putting away the leftover pizza, Ben follows me in.

"Don't you want any more pizza?"

I shake my head.

He sits next to me on the bed. To his credit, he doesn't tell me everything's going to be fine. "How's the other woman doing, Elizabeth?"

"Isabel. Fine, I think. No one's said anything and I haven't been re-quarantined, so she must be fine, right?"

"Right. And we only have Leo—Lincoln's WHISP—to compare yours to, so the differences might not mean anything. I was thinking that since you and Lincoln were related they'd be similar, but you both got your WHISPs under very different circumstances, so I don't know why I was thinking that. You're unique and so is he." He kisses my temple. "I'm sorry for worrying you about all this."

Unsure of whether he's just trying to make me feel better, I nuzzle his neck. I guess that's fine for right now.

———

LATER, UNABLE TO DRIFT OFF, I SNEAK INTO THE kitchen for some more pizza. Liv's shadow in the dark glass of the microwave jumpstarts my heart with a painful jolt. I avert my gaze from the reflection. "Stop doing that." I'm not sure if I'm talking to her or myself, but then my anger ignites. "You things are ruining everything, you know." I imagine a WHISP-less world, blissfully normal without fear of the unknown literally following me wherever I go. The microwave beeps and I rush to pull out the pizza without looking at the door. "The world is weird and horrible and complicated enough, we don't need you making things worse." Sitting, I take a bite and have to hold my mouth open to prevent the molten cheese from burning the roof of my mouth. I wonder if the WHISP particles around Liv's invisible mouth are swirling in agitation from the phantom heat.

Eventually, the pizza is cool enough to swallow. *Stop thinking about it. Sending more brain waves that way is only making it stronger and strengthening the bond.* Probably, but I've tried for almost a year to pretend Liv doesn't exist, and it hasn't worked yet. "Maybe if you were more useful." Another bite. "If you could do the laundry or the dishes, you know, earn your keep." It occurs to me then that she does do the dishes and the laundry already, every time I do them. Since Liv doesn't eat or wear clothes, that must be really frustrating. I picture her more like a teenage me and try out a huffy accent. "Why do I have to wash dishes? I don't even eat food?"

"Who are you talking to?"

I choke on my pizza and whip me head around to a blurry-eyed Ben standing in the doorway. Coughing, I finally manage to whisper, "No one."

CHAPTER 19

Excerpt from Transcript of Session 41:
Dr. Aziz Fritz with Det. S. Harbinger

Fritz: You're quiet today.
Harbinger: I assume you heard about the bombing.
Fritz: In Turkey? Yes, I did.
Harbinger: I'm just really hoping the U.S. government doesn't
suggest all-WHISP neighborhoods.
Fritz: I heard there are WHISP-only communities already, partic-
ularly in the Southwest.
Harbinger: Yeah, I heard that, too.
Fritz: What do you think about them?
Harbinger: I think they're a bad idea, judging by what happened
in Turkey.

I'M IN SOME KIND OF LABORATORY STRAPPED DOWN
to an operating table. Liv is on the table next to me, but it
doesn't seem strange that she's next to me instead of behind
me. Figures in hazmat suits wander around the lab with
beakers and clipboards as I struggle with my bonds. Then one

approaches with a large, serrated knife and looks from me to Liv before taking the knife to Liv's shoulder. Heart pounding, I awake with echoes of her screams in my ears. No, just the alarm. I slap it off. Beside me, Ben is still snoring softly. As the room comes into focus and the nightmare fades, my chest aches. My nightmare is over, but what about the kidnap victims? It's time to stop chasing videos and cold cyber-trails. CAW might not be involved in this crime, but they've done similar crimes in the past. They must know something.

EVEN THOUGH I'M CERTAIN I WON'T RUN INTO ANY other WHISPers at CAW headquarters, it's still a bad idea for me to storm into their offices. Instead, I call Lila Grant and ask her to come down to the precinct for a chat. To my surprise, she accepts, but when we sit down in the conference room an hour later, she slides a request for the return of McCaffrey's computer across the table. Ah, that explains it.

"If I told you we needed it to track the people trying to frame CAW, would you let us keep it another week?"

She tilts her head in a gesture Grumps, our cat, would be proud of. "Are you?"

"We are, in fact."

She pulls the paper back and slips it into her briefcase. "Okay, you have until the end of the week." She rises.

"Whoa there, my turn."

Checking her watch, she sighs and sits. "What can I help you with, Detective?"

There are many ways I could start this conversation. I choose one of the least antagonistic. "I understand that CAW no longer engages in alleged illegal activities, but let's say for a moment that you used to."

"Before I say anything, let me remind you that the contract you previously signed assures CAW immunity for any information shared for five years. This entire conversation with you falls under that previously signed contract."

"Okay, fine. That makes this easier, then. When CAW was mutilating people with WHISPs, you must've had a team of—using the term loosely—researchers. Assuming these programs are no longer active, what happened to those researchers?"

She doesn't meet my eye. "Well, some of those researchers may still be with CAW in other capacities or continuing to examine data previously collected."

I knew they weren't completely legit. "And the others?"

"Others may not have agreed with CAW's new trajectory and left the organization."

"And gone where? Don't tell me you haven't been watching—"

"The DOD."

I blink. "The Department of Defense."

"At least one of our former doctors, Dr. Levi Samuels, is now under contract with the Department of Defense. A second doctor, Dr. Michael Higgins, left the country shortly after separating from CAW. We lost track of him when he entered Georgia. It's my understanding that WHISP research there is largely unfettered by ethics regulations."

Dead ends? "Is there anything you can tell me about the underground WHISP testing world that might help with this investigation? You must've known other players, maybe even conferred with another organization?"

"I've seen a lot of things in the past few years, but if this organization is really working on some sort of WHISP bioweapon, that's new to me and I'm sure they didn't expect for this little test or whatever it was to be found out as something more than a kidnapping. You're welcome. Mostly, this type of research falls into the same dubious research done by stem cell research companies, for instance. I think you would be surprised at the size of the black market medical and laboratory economy. We had little trouble making largely untraceable cash purchases for most anything we thought we needed."

"I don't suppose you could get me in contact with any of those suppliers?"

She traces her upper lip with her index finger. "Maybe. It would all have to be anonymous, of course. I assume you're looking for similar purchases as we would've made."

"Yeah, but they wouldn't be likely to disclose who those purchases were from, now would they?"

"True, and honestly, we did most of our purchasing as an anonymous source, so they might not know who was making the purchase."

I lean back in my chair. "Then really, what useful information would they be able to give me?"

Grant shrugs. "Perhaps nothing. Do you still want me to see if I can make a connection?"

Another depressing thought takes over. "What incentive would your ex-supplier have to help NYPD put away one of their customers?"

"I was also wondering that."

Another thought springs up. Uh oh. This could go spectacularly awry. "If CAW really is changing their ways, then you wouldn't need to be on good terms with a shady provider of lab equipment, would you?"

She narrows her eyes. "What are you getting at, Detective?"

"A sting."

———

THE CHIEF REMOVES HIS GLASSES AND RUBS THE

bridge of his nose. "Okay, Harbinger, run me through this again."

"CAW places an order with their dodgy laboratory equipment supplier and NYPD, maybe with CompUServer Plus's help, monitors the transaction. If we can't trace the supplier through the order, we work with CAW in a sting operation during the delivery of the merchandise."

"And we're just hoping this is the same supplier of equipment to the kidnappers of our case?"

"Or that they'll have information about another supplier or another order, or have heard something about a bioweapon."

He shakes his head. "We won't have much to hold them on or threaten them with. Not properly collecting state sales tax? I'm pretty sure they'll claim to be a legitimate supplier of equipment who has no idea what their equipment is used for, especially if we can't prove the equipment is stolen."

I've got a plan for that. "That's why we have CAW order something illegal in their order, like drugs, or explosives, something that requires permits and licensure that CAW doesn't have."

"Green, what's your take?"

She purses her lips. "Could work."

The Chief frowns. "But do we need this? Where are we with our other leads?"

Green holds up a hand and ticks off fingers. "No trace recovered from the crime scene, warehouse, or van, except Rondell McCaffrey's fingerprint, and we're now pretty sure that was planted. We haven't been able to trace the white van to the crime scene or the Radcliffe Imports truck once it reached Jersey. And, while CompUServer Plus is still working on the hacking redirection trace, the first reroute took them to an IP address in Saudi Arabia."

"How many of those reroutes could there be?"

She shrugs. "They say there's usually an average of five to seven."

I butt back in. "But even if they find the original IP address, there's every indication that it could be another shell company like Radcliffe Imports and get us nowhere."

Green sniffs. "How do we know this supplier will even work with CAW again? Haven't they supposedly been quiet in their illegal experiment department for a while?"

Green's not wrong. "Hopefully, they didn't place weekly orders. Also, we'll throw some new equipment requests in there to make the supplier think CAW's working on a new project."

The Chief gives me a hard look. "You know I don't like the idea of us working with CAW, particularly *you* working with CAW."

My gut churns. "I know, but it has to be me. I'm the only one who's signed a confidentiality agreement with them."

He puts his hand to his mouth and drags it down over his chin. "All right. But let's be smart about this, people. The press would be all over this, and if this supplier gets any inkling that NYPD is working with CAW, this whole thing is a bust. Green, I want you to work with Beaulieu to get everything we need to work the phone or internet trace, or however CAW is going to make contact. If it's via the internet, see if she can rope in more help from CompUServer Plus, too. Harbinger, smooth the way with your CAW contacts for Green and Beaulieu, and talk to your buddy McCaffrey."

"Why McCaffrey?"

"He's head of their public relations, right? See if he'll do a press release about NYPD's bias against CAW and how badly he was treated by us while in custody. Maybe even have him accuse us of mishandling evidence."

"Is that really a good idea? I'm not sure the task force needs any more bad press right now."

He shrugs. "Hopefully, people will consider the source, and if all goes to plan, later it'll come out that we were working with CAW."

Great. How often does anything go to plan? "Is that any better press? Us working with CAW?"

His mouth turns up at the corners in a grim smile. "I hear they're turning over a new leaf."

CHAPTER 20

Excerpt from Transcript of Session 28:
Dr. Aziz Fritz with Det. S. Harbinger

Harbinger: I'm starting to have doubts about joining the task force.
Fritz: Oh?
Harbinger: I don't want the media to turn it into some kind of WHISP witch hunt.
Fritz: Are you afraid that your presence will skew media opinion about it?
Harbinger: It's not like I'm the greatest WHISP poster child.
Fritz: Perhaps not.

BY THAT EVENING, MCCAFFREY HAS DONE HIS PART and released a pretty scathing report of his interactions with the NYPD. I'm guessing he didn't have to stretch himself too much to write it. Although, come on, we find your fingerprint in the vehicle used in a crime, we're going to arrest you. He named me specifically, which wasn't necessarily part of the plan, but since I'm the only one on the task force with a WHISP, it made sense. We decided to postpone the deal with the equipment supplier until tomorrow so it seems slightly less suspicious, and I'm just packing up when my cell buzzes. It's Lincoln calling. I sit back down.

"Hey kid."

"Mom. How are you?"

"I'm okay, how're you doing? Sorry you're kicked out of your own apartment right now."

"Don't worry about it. Listen, I don't know if you've seen the news tonight, but—"

"I know. It's not what it looks like."

"But this guy is calling for an investigation into your behavior. Could that get you kicked off the task force?"

"No. It's not…" What if someone in the media like that bitch Janet Williams tries to interview Lincoln about this? How good would he be at lying? *Shit.* "It's not that bad."

"Not that bad? Mom, have you seen the news? And after that other report… Are you still on the case?"

"Geez, first they think NYPD is working with CAW, now they think we're wrongfully attacking CAW, I wish they'd make up their minds."

"I'm serious."

The worry in his voice makes me cringe. "I know, I'm sorry. Yes, I'm still on the case. Things might get a little bad for a while, but this isn't strangers from the FBI calling the shots, it's the Chief, and I didn't actually do anything wrong this time."

"I'm just worried about you."

"I know." Is he overly worried? "Did you and your dad get the results back from my new measurements?"

Silence.

"Lincoln."

"You've been under a lot of stress with this case. There are too many variables."

"That bad, huh?"

"I don't know what Dad said, but we don't even know what we're looking for. This data is all so preliminary, it's ridiculous. But, the more data we have, the better, so I want to keep doing the measurements, but don't worry about them, okay?"

My cop sense tingles and I'm not sure if he believes what he's telling me, but I do want him to think he's making me feel better. "Okay." I struggle to find something more to say. "Tell your friend we really owe her. What's her name again?"

"Naomi, and she's just a colleague."

"Have I met her before?"

"Maybe when you visited the lab."

Having no idea who the woman is, I grab at straws. "Is she the tall one with the dark hair?"

He chuckles. "No. And I know what you're doing. We're just friends."

"Oooo, upgraded from colleagues now."

"Argh. Funny. You're sure you're okay?"

"Yes, I'm okay. We might even be making some progress in the case soon."

"Good." A pause. "Well, I'll let you go. I just wanted to make sure you were okay."

He's a good kid. "Thanks. I love you."

"Love you, too."

"Bye." *Kiddo.*

"Bye."

———

WHEN WE MEET IN THE LAB AGAIN, I HAVE A SIMILAR conversation with Ben over the Indian food he picked up. Having played poker with my husband, I also don't mention to him that the press release is a sham. It at least fooled two people.

"No, seriously, Sylvy, I'm really sick of the press bad-mouthing you. Don't they have anything better to do? And I've seen almost nothing about the shelter kidnapping. Don't you think they should be more concerned with trying to help find out what happened to those people? Maybe NYPD should work with the media more on this case. You could appeal to the public for tips. You're still looking for the Radcliffe Imports truck, right?"

I'm not sure Ben realizes the flood of phone calls generated by a public appeal like that and the amount of cop-power it takes to run down all those leads, ninety-nine percent of which are worthless.

"Maybe it's better the media hasn't done more coverage. For one, we don't want to start a city-wide panic about a possible bioweapon. Can you imagine the circus that would spring up if they got wind of that? And two, since the truck left the city, a local news report won't really help us track it down."

He swallows down some goat biryani. "You're right. I just wish they were helping things rather than fanning flames, you know."

If only you knew. "I know."

"And the Chief is behind you for sure?"

I finish a large piece of naan topped with butter chicken. "Yes. I didn't actually do anything wrong this time." *Why is that so hard for everyone to believe?*

"Right, right. I'm sorry. Of course, you didn't."

"It's fine. We don't need them. I think we might get a break in the case soon."

He heaps more rice onto a piece of naan. "Oh?"

"Yep."

———

THE CONTACT BETWEEN CAW AND THE SUPPLIER IS supposed to take place around ten in the morning, but not exactly at ten, so by ten-fifteen, I'm sitting at my desk, chewing on my thumbnail, and waiting for a text from Lila Grant. Every flaw in this plan has been running through my mind since I set my head on the pillow last night and failed to sleep: CAW could mess up the contact on purpose or give themselves away by accident, the supplier could just not want to deal with them right now because of McCaffrey's recent arrest, the supplier could legitimately not be able to get their hands on the controlled substances we're asking them for, or everything could go smoothly with the contact, only to fall apart when we try to catch the supplier at the equipment drop. My idea. No pressure.

My phone buzzes and I slosh coffee onto my desk. At least, it's not on my pants. It's Grant.

Grant: Made contact. Awaiting reply.

So helpful.

Harbinger: Kk

Green is over with Beaulieu at CompUServer Plus supposedly monitoring the exchange. I text her.

Harbinger: Well?

Her reply takes a few minutes.

Green: Nothing yet. Exchange is private chat window in forum. Trace not looking good.

Harbinger: Thx. Keep me in loop.

Crap. Well, tracking the supplier down through their contact with CAW was always going to be a bit of a longshot. The important thing would be to lure them into a drop off of the equipment. For previous orders, most of the time, CAW would retrieve equipment from one of two locations, a wharf currently in receivership, or under an overpass in Harlem. As of now, we have eyes on both locations, but if they chose to deliver to a third and only let CAW know a short time before the drop off, we'll have a much tougher time boxing them in without them knowing and bailing. Again, no pressure.

Having no idea when the supplier will get back in touch with Grant, I try and fail to focus on more background checking of the victims. I want to pace the length of the department, but my stomach's decided to protest the three cups of coffee and half a bagel I had for breakfast, so instead I rest my head on my desk. This doesn't settle my stomach, but does produce a throbbing in my temple.

"Sleeping on the job again?"

I open my eyes to find Crone in front of my desk. I pick up my head more to relieve the ache than as a courtesy to him and lean back in my chair. "Well, I didn't sleep at home, so I've gotta do it somewhere, right?"

"Heard you guys had somethin' big going on today, but obviously, I was misinformed."

"Is that really why you're here or did you finally decide to drop off your application for the task force?"

Crone snorts. "I also heard you might be getting kicked off the case again, so I thought I'd lend you a shoulder to drink on."

Chuckling, I shake my head. "I appreciate that, but really, I'm fine, and I'm not getting kicked off the case, so don't worry."

"All right. All right. Just trying to be nice, forget I said anything. What've you guys got cookin' today, anyway?"

"Sorry, can't say. If only you were on the task force."

"Whatever." He turns away. Halfway to the elevator he calls back over his shoulder, "And I was going to bring you a donut from the break room."

"Sure you were!"

My cell phone buzzes again. It's Grant.

Grant: Order accepted. Drop off will be the underpass. Will let you know time.

Harbinger: Thumbs-up emoji.

Okay, now we're in business.

CHAPTER 21

Excerpt from Transcript of Session 58:
Dr. Aziz Fritz with Det. S. Harbinger

Harbinger: Sorry I'm late.
Fritz: No worries. How are you doing?
Harbinger: Not great.
Fritz: I'm listening.
Harbinger: Another death threat came to the precinct today.
Fritz: Another threat against you?
Harbinger: No. This one was addressed to the Chief.
Fritz: Because he's the head of the task force?
Harbinger: Yeah. Sucks.

AFTER A SLEEPLESS NIGHT, A LUNCH OF PAIN MEDS, A
power bar, a Coke, and a whole afternoon of waiting for a sting
I won't be a part of, my stomach is a cauldron of malcontent
and my nerves are raw and ragged. I've got the best
surveillance view of the underpass queued up on my computer,
but it's not the same. Not only would the Chief not let me go
because a number of homeless in the area have WHISPs, but
also, since I was named in the press release, I might have media

eyes on me. It doesn't matter that I agree with him or that I think I might throw up at any moment, I'm still irritated. The fact that I'm the only person left behind in the basement tonight (and Ben's constantly texting to ask when I'll be home) doesn't help.

My gaze is glued to the grainy image on the screen when an unmarked truck pulls into view. The CAW vehicle parked in the shadows of the underpass flashes its lights twice, and the truck responds by flashing its lights in quick succession. As I watch, Grant exits the CAW vehicle with a briefcase and walks to a point halfway between the two vehicles. She sets down the briefcase and retreats several paces. Two men emerge from the truck, one with an automatic weapon slung over his shoulder. *Shit. Shit. Shit.* Grant didn't mention automatic weapons. It's hard to tell from the poor quality of the video if she's surprised by the weapon.

A pang of sympathy hits my chest for her. I didn't think she'd actually be risking her life for us. The plan was to stop the truck on its way out after the exchange, but with an automatic in play, I'm not sure what plan B is. Grant doesn't hold up her hands, but points to the briefcase and appears to be talking calmly. The man with the weapon doesn't brandish it as the other man goes to the briefcase and flips it open on the ground. After a cursory examination of the contents, he closes it, stands, and gives a thumbs up to the truck. Two more men exit the truck and walk around to the back. A few moments later, they return carrying a large crate between them. They deposit the crate roughly where the briefcase had been and Grant nods.

All the men are returning to the truck when Grant dives behind the crate and all hell breaks loose. As shots take out its tires, the truck suddenly sags. At the same moment, SWAT and police swarm in from every direction. The man with the automatic brings it up only to be taken down before he's able to fire. The man with the briefcase only makes it to the truck door before shots rain into it and he stops and raises his hands. One of the other two men runs toward Grant and the crate, while the other drops to his knees in place. Bitterness floods my mouth as the man reaches the crate. *Run Lila!* But then I nearly laugh out loud when the man rounds the crate and Grant has a gun in her steady hands pointed at his head. Seconds later, officers close in on them both. Only when the man is handcuffed does Grant relinquish her gun to one of the officers.

I should've known she could take care of herself. My shoulders come down from around my ears, but then the truck is in motion heading toward the crate and Grant and picking up speed despite its blown tires. *Oh fuck!* Still behind the crate, she can't see the truck, but she must be able to hear it because she bolts for the cover of one of the overpass pillars as gunfire erupts again, shattering the truck's windows and causing sparks to dance over its white surface. My heart is in my mouth as the officer who took Grant's gun dives out from under the truck's tire as it smashes through the crate then continues right through and crashes into the CAW SUV. *Oh, I really hope no one was still in that car.* The truck starts to back up, and more gunfire erupts from police. My guts tie into a knot thinking of the number of potentially lethal ricochets.

Finally, the truck rolls to a stop, the driver's side door opens, and a bloody woman falls out onto the ground. On the video, everything stops and the dust thrown up from the truck swirls in the air for what seems like almost a minute. Then SWAT is on the truck, their black forms like ants on a lollipop. About a minute and a half later, I recognize an all-clear signal and feel like I could ooze out of my chair onto the floor. It's over. Now, let's hope it was worth it.

———

FOR A TENSE HOUR AND A HALF, I WATCH THE aftermath of the exchange on my computer. Ambulances and firetrucks arrive and one ambulance departs within minutes, likely with the gunman and/or the woman driving the truck. So far, I don't see any body bags. It'll probably take another hour, at least, to process the uninjured arrests, which means I've got a while before interviews. My stomach growls. Now that the adrenaline of the sting is gone, my belly is gnawing at my backbone. I'm tempted to ask Ben to bring me food, but there's still some guilt from lying to him earlier, and he was a little mad when I told him I couldn't go into the lab for more measurements tonight but couldn't give him a good reason.

Despite my hunger, nothing sounds appealing, so I just go with a pizza place open late that I know delivers to the precinct, and shoot off an order for two larges, one meat and one veggie. If the others on the task force have already eaten, then at least I'll have some emergency leftovers at the precinct for the next few days. My phone buzzes. It's Green.

Green: Well, that didn't go to plan.

Harbinger: I saw. Any casualties?

Green: Clemont got friendly fire in his shoulder. Lady driver died on way to hospital. Guy with gun critical. Nothing else major.

Harbinger: Grant pissed?

Green: Oh yeah.

Harbinger: I ordered pizza.

Green: Mouth-watering emoji.

Harbinger: ETA?

Green: Half hour?

Harbinger: Thumbs up emoji.

Setting the phone down, I consider our approach for the interview. I guess I was expecting nerdier criminals to be selling black market lab equipment. *Duh.* We've got them selling illegal drugs, but that's pretty weak considering we shot two of their crew and killed one of them. Also, with the bust, their business is done in New York City, at least for a while. I would've preferred to keep this whole thing out of the papers, but there is no way a shootout like that involving NYPD won't be a front-page story. Here's hoping the Chief can use his near magical skills to obfuscate what really went on. I'm guessing his cover will be a drug ring bust, but if anyone recognized Grant at the scene, we're screwed. If not, maybe we can leverage keeping who we actually busted out of the media. Keeping things quiet might, at least, protect the seller's black market lab equipment selling rep until the drug charges are settled.

Still, I have a bad feeling about this. The whole goal was to have just enough leverage over the equipment sellers to ease them into talking. Now, having killed one of their own, all we can expect is animosity. It seems like the worst outcome possible, and I'm struggling hard to find an angle. *Damnit. Can maybe just one thing go right with this case?* Rage coats my throat with heat, but also guilt. This was all my idea, and someone died. Maybe not a great person, maybe even a person who tried to use a truck to mow down my fellow officers, but still, I put her in that position. And for what? If her friends aren't willing to talk, then nothing.

My desk phone jangles to life. "Harbinger."

"There's a delivery for you."

"Yeah, thanks. Be right up. Um, the delivery person doesn't have a WHISP, do they?"

"No?"

"Good. I'll be right up." Almost forgot I could be some kind of WHISP reaper, though really, would a bioweapon take this long to activate?

I speed up the stairs, but am more cautious on the main floor. There's still a fair amount of activity for this time of night and I don't want to accidentally run into anyone I could potentially infect. However, the coast is clear all the way to the front desk where a scrawny teen with shaggy black hair, wearing far too few layers for the bitter weather, waits, two pizza boxes stacked on the desk in front of him. When I approach with my wallet out, his face changes from bored to something unsettling.

"How much do I owe you?"

"You're her."

"Excuse me?"

He gestures to my WHISP. "You're the cop from the news. The one stickin' it to CAW." He makes a lude movement with his fist.

"Um…"

"My bro has a WHISP and my uncle, too. We're behind you." He holds up his hand, palm facing me, face expectant.

Just no. I nod and hold out twenty-five dollars cash instead. "Here, yeah thanks. Keep the change."

After an awkward pause, he takes the money. "Well, keep up the good work." He pumps his fist again as his eyes stray to Liv.

A trickle of ice water drips down my spine. This kid is into WHISPs in a not entirely healthy way. *Ick.* "Yeah, okay." I want to back away, so Liv doesn't get any closer to him, but there isn't any way to do it, so I grab the pizza boxes, turn and powerwalk, trying not to think about how uncomfortable the kid's stare is making me. When I enter the security of the stairwell, I shudder. This is an entirely new experience and an entirely unpleasant one. *Why right now?* It's not like I'm under any stress as it is. Heat from the pizzas searing my hands, I head down and deposit them in our sad little excuse for a break room, which is actually just a table cluttered with a coffee pot, coffee, creamer, sugar, and mugs and a mini-fridge underneath it next to another table with chairs around it. Plunking down in one of the chairs, I open the first box, but my enthusiasm for the pizza within has waned. I grab a slice anyway and force myself to eat. I'll be useless in the interview if I pass out from hunger.

———

EVEN BEFORE WE ENTER THE INTERROGATION ROOM, I have a bad feeling. I don't know what exactly it is about the man in the room, but he rubs me the wrong way before I even speak to him. What we know is that his name is Nazil Kurisaqila and he's originally from Fiji. He's got one prior arrest for theft, but otherwise his slate is clean. His last known legitimate job was as a hospital orderly, which is probably how he got involved in the illicit sales of medical equipment. Green's been watching him for about five minutes when she turns to me.

"We gotta play this asshole hard or he's not going to give us anything."

"I agree. Maybe he's fond of his sparkling record. We could use that against him. Tell him a big fat drug charge will look pretty ugly on it."

Green bites her lower lip. "Maybe."

I shrug. "I'll follow your lead."

She nods once. "Right."

We head into the interrogation room and as soon as we open the door, Nazil is yanking at his cuffs where they're secured to the table.

"This is bullshit! I want my law— What the fuck is that? I didn't even think cops were allowed to have those fucking things! I want my lawyer and she needs to get the fuck out!"

Well, this is a first. I've had a lot of people hate Liv, look at me like I'm a leper because of her, but I've never seen a grown man like Nazil so afraid of her...of me. Perspective hits me like a lightning bolt. *Was I this obvious and awful with my fear?* I open my mouth but can't find anything to say. We were planning on going at Nazil hard, but if I stay, I can only see a civil suit: psychological police brutality. Once again, my purpose is negated by the shadow at my back and it stings, but I retreat to the corridor and close the door. Green's muffled voice intermingles with Nazil's.

"You okay?"

Not sure how long I've been standing here. I meet the Chief's gaze. "Yeah. It just...sucks."

He nods, then lifts his chin in the direction of the observation room.

I follow him in.

CHAPTER 22

Excerpt from Transcript of Session 48:
Dr. Aziz Fritz with Det. S. Harbinger

Fritz: We haven't talked about your WHISP directly in several sessions. Has anything changed?
Harbinger: Changed?
Fritz: Yes. Any new experiences? Sensations?
Harbinger: I almost got into an accident when I caught a glimpse of it in the rearview mirror the other day. Does that count?
Fritz: All right. Any new positive experiences?
Harbinger: Like what?
Fritz: Have you started to feel any connection to your WHISP?
Harbinger: In what way would that be a positive thing?

WE'RE ON OUR LAST INTERVIEW AND OUR LAST SHOT to make something out of this terrific, expensive, deadly gamble I've gotten us into. It's pushing midnight, but with all the drama of the day, I'm wide awake and wired tighter than a new piano. The man in interrogation now, Wayne Vasco, is our best hope to get any information. He was the money man, and has a much longer rap sheet than any of the others: fraud, embezzlement, check forging, and a myriad of other white collar crimes. Few charges of which stuck and none that resulted in prison time. His slick, mousy brown hair, watery eyes, and slippery demeanor complete the persona of an insurance weasel. Green and I don't even have to discuss it. His oily confidence will be his undoing.

When we enter the interrogation room, he's already bristling with indignation.

"This is outrageous. I'm a legitimate businessman trying to make a simple transaction and you're shooting at us? I'll have all of your badges by 8 a.m."

I let out a breath as I sit down next to Green on the other side of the table. He hasn't even flinched at my WHISP. "Mr. Vasco, I'm Detective Harbinger and this is Detective Green. I'm sorry to have to tell you this, but legitimate businessmen don't traffic in illegal drugs."

"It was my understanding that those drugs were to be used in scientific experimentation along with the provided lab equipment."

"Even if the recipient of those drugs had the proper permits, which they don't, you, Mr. Vasco, are not an authorized and licensed supplier of illegal drugs."

He makes a motion with his restrained hands like he's waving away a fly. "I'm just the middleman. I didn't have any idea what this particular delivery consisted of, and I assumed the appropriate parties had provided appropriate paperwork and licensure on both sides of the transaction."

Green shows her teeth. "I thought you just said it was your understanding that the drugs were going to be used in scientific experiments. How could that have been your understanding if you didn't know the shipment contained drugs?"

A crack in his smooth facade appears in the form of an eye twitch. "Well, I—"

I flip open his file. "You seem to have a lot of misunderstandings when it comes to the law and what's legal and what isn't."

He clears his throat. "My past may seem slightly checkered, but as I'm sure you can also tell from my file, most of those misunderstandings were cleared up."

Green takes over again. "So, we have the illegal drug charges, the conspiracy to sell illegal drugs, collaboration in the shooting of a police officer, and endangerment charges as well as CAW's testimony regarding the purchase of a number of other stolen and illegal items from you and your organization over the past several years. I think with your past record, any lawyer will have a hard time keeping you out of prison this time." She turns to me. "What do you think, Harbinger, six, seven years?"

"Oh, I think the officer shooting bumps it to at least ten." It helps that in all the chaos, Vasco has no idea his partner with the assault rifle never got off a shot.

Vasco's sleek brows find his hairline. "Ten years? That's ridiculous. People don't get ten years for police mistakes. I'm sure my partner was simply defending himself. How was he to know it was the police? He probably thought it was a gang raid."

Green shakes her head. "A gang raid? Is he hard of hearing? Because I'm sure we have a recording of an officer shouting, 'This is the police, put your weapon on the ground.'"

"Ten years, seven years, the point is you, Mr. Vasco, are looking at hard time this time around. And let me tell you, you don't want any part of that."

Green nods. "Not to mention, the loss of *legitimate* business a lengthy jail term would mean."

His gaze flits from Green back to me, calculating. "Is there some kind of deal on the table?"

I'm so glad this guy has a heart of flint. If he actually cared about the death of the woman driving the truck, we wouldn't be here right now. Also, I'm glad Green is good at making up bogus charges. Sure, if someone is killed during the commission of a crime, all parties involved in the crime are responsible, but with an injury, the law gets much muddier. Not to mention that Clemont's injury came from friendly fire. All we really have Vasco on are the drug charges, and a good lawyer could probably get him off somehow. "Well, there might be, but it's a longshot. There's another case we're working on, and the DA may be able to see her way through to more leniency if you provided a solid lead for us in that case."

"How could I help you with another case?"

"We're looking for an organization other than CAW who might have used your services recently. They would've purchased items such as these." I pull out a list put together by CAW and the task force with Ben's help. On it are collapsible stretchers, hazmat suits, and tranquilizers, as well as Faraday cages and particle measuring equipment. Watching his face closely, I slide the paper over to him and almost scream with relief when recognition floods his eyes as he reads.

He frowns and looks up. "I want full immunity, not just no jail time. I want to be a free man in the next twelve hours. Whatever happened tonight never happened, and I wasn't involved."

Way to throw your partners or employees or whatever under the bus. "I can't make promises until I talk to the DA, and this pass is only valid if your information bears fruit for our investigation."

"Oh, come on. I can't promise you that. I can only give you what I have."

"And if you have a solid lead for us that checks out, we might have a deal. Let us talk to the DA, get papers drawn up. You can choose whether or not you want to sign them." Green and I rise. "In the meantime, you'll be escorted back to holding." Won't hurt to give him a little taste of prison. The DA,

Adrianna Leverman, is already on board, of course. That was the whole point of this sting. She's not going to like letting this bastard off the hook, especially in light of the shit-show the arrest became, but she also knows Vasco would probably get off anyway. This way, we can also throw in a clause preventing him from bringing a civil suit against the NYPD, though if the woman or the gunman have any close family, we'll likely be getting one from each of them.

When we reach the door, Vasco calls to our backs, "How long is this going to take?"

Green shrugs.

I purse my lips. "We won't know until we wake her up."

———

"WE WON'T KNOW UNTIL WE WAKE HER UP?" Adrianna shakes her head at me. "Bold, Harbinger, bold."

"No, not bold. If this guy gets an inkling this whole thing's a setup, we could be screwed."

"How much more could he ask for? Return of the cash from CAW's order?"

I grin. "No, but he could've wised up, taken his chance in court, and given us nothing."

"Thank God, he's too stupid to ask for a lawyer."

I want to share Green's optimism, but I won't feel comfortable until he signs the paper. "Bite your tongue. He could change his mind about that." And then there's still the possibility that his lead will be Radcliffe Imports or something equally useless. *Way to focus on the positive, Sylvy.*

We sit in silence for around twenty-five minutes, Adrianna checking her phone and Green perusing Vasco's extensive file. I get up and walk around the first floor of the precinct, too edgy to focus on anything productive. After another fifteen minutes, I finally crack and reenter the observation room.

"Do you think enough time has passed?"

Adrianna checks her watch. "Yeah, okay, let's bring him back in."

My adrenaline is beginning to fade and my eyelids droop. Rubbing them, all I want is a hot shower and maybe a four-hour nap, but I nod. "Come on, Green, let's do this."

———

Keeping my face deadpan as Vasco signs the plea bargain isn't hard considering my lack of sleep this past week, yet I'm afraid he'll hear my rabbiting heart over the scratching of the pen. He drops the pen on the table and, having been freed from his handcuffs, stretches his arms above his head. Green leans over and drags the paper and pen back to our side of the table to make sure everything's in order and I poise my pen over a clean sheet of legal pad. It's all come down to this. *Oh please, oh please, oh please.* "Okay, Vasco, tell us what you've got."

"Can I get something to eat first? I'm a little peckish. Maybe a nice ribeye with a glass of chianti?" He chuckles.

An urge to strangle him gradually subsides. "One, I think you've seen too many movies, two, you should've added NYPD providing you with dinner into your deal, and three, your status as a free man rests on the information you provide to us right now, so I think I'd just start talking, if I were you."

His stupid grin evaporates. "Fine. I remember this order, mainly because of the narcotics blend they asked for." He stops. "For which they had all of the proper licensure and we, um—"

"It's fine. We aren't trying to rope you for another drug charge. Just tell us about the purchaser."

He lets out a breath. "It's not like I have a name. That's not the way this works. It's anonymity and cash that keep my business going."

"So you really have nothing for us? This isn't looking like you're fulfilling your end of the bargain, Vasco." I set the pen down.

"No, I don't have a name, but I can do better. I have a location."

"A location?"

Green snorts. "Do you expect us to believe they had you drop off narcotics at their doorstep?"

"No. But with all new orders, we take certain precautions."

With what happened today, I find that hard to believe, but then again, this wasn't a new order. "What kind of precautions?"

"Well, for one, we have the buyer send half the money ahead of time to an overseas bank account, and then there's the tracker."

Now he's got my attention. "Tracker?"

"So, it's not like we can count all the money right there. I mean, I have a pretty good eye for cash stacks, but sometimes people sneak tens into stacks of twenties or fives into stacks of hundreds."

"I get the idea."

"Anyway, we insert a tracker into the container so we can recoup our money if they try to short us."

"And there was a tracker in this order?"

"A-yep. But they didn't short us, so I didn't activate it."

My fists clench. "But you still can."

"Just need access to a computer."

Ignoring the smug smirk hanging on Vasco's face, I look to Green. Her face says it all: Now we're in business.

CHAPTER 23

Excerpt from Transcript of Session 23:
Dr. Aziz Fritz with Det. S. Harbinger

*Harbinger: At least now I have something in common with
my son.*
Fritz: You didn't feel like you had any common ground before?
*Harbinger: Not really. Even before he had a WHISP, he's always
taken after Ben. Science is his thing, not law enforcement.*
Fritz: He could've taken up forensic science.
*Harbinger: Sorry, you're right, physics is his thing. Plus, I think
it's kinda hard for a kid to have a cop as a parent.*
Fritz: How so?
*Harbinger: Most kids don't have to worry about their parents
getting shot at work.*

AS TIRED AS I AM, VASCO'S POSSIBLE ABILITY TO
track the kidnappers is like a shot of adrenaline right in my
heart. Before I can blink, Beaulieu is in the interrogation room
with a laptop connected to several black boxes, one with anten-
nae. Green and I crowd behind Vasco who sighs heavily and

mutters under his breath about needing to reroute his system after this, but his fingers start flying across the keyboard.

"But seriously, can I get a hamburger or something?"

Green frowns but goes to the door and chats with the officer there about an order from YahtzeeBurger.

"No onions!"

Green rolls her eyes in Vasco's direction.

Screens flash past in quick succession, and I'm clueless, but Beaulieu is nodding as Vasco navigates from screen to screen. Finally, he pauses and cracks his knuckles.

"There. Activated. But it'll take a few minutes for the GPS to ping the satellites." He pokes one of the black boxes attached to the laptop. "I can get you the latest model of that, half off, even."

Beaulieu shows her teeth. "Thanks, but we recently signed an equipment contract with CompUServer Plus."

As he shrugs, I stifle a punch-drunk giggle.

A minute passes in anticipatory silence.

"Soooo. What's this case anyway?"

"We can't discuss an active investigation."

Vasco snorts. "Whatever." Then he turns to look at me. Me and Liv. "Wait, fuck. This is that kidnapping, isn't it? You're that Detective from the news." He turns back to the computer screen. "Shit. I should've asked for a fucking reward."

Green shakes her head. "Your freedom is your reward."

"If you say so."

There's a flicker on the screen and a series of numbers come up.

"That's it." Beaulieu nudges Vasco's hands away, copies the numbers, and brings up a new tab. A map of the eastern seaboard appears, then magnifies down to New York State and New Jersey, then magnifies down to New York State only, then magnifies down to upstate New York, then magnifies down to a single red dot in roughly the middle of nowhere.

The kidnappers could have dumped the crates out in the middle of a field somewhere to throw us off, but how could they've known one of the crates had a tracking device? This is no trail of breadcrumbs. If the equipment is there, the kidnap victims should be there, too.

Green pats my shoulder. "Can you coordinate with the local and state cops?"

"Absolutely." The victims all have WHISPs, and are probably all infected with some kind of WHISP disease; there is no way I can go, yet I'm itching to jump in Green's car again. "Where is that, Beaulieu?"

"Nearest listed is Madawaska, but I don't think they have a police unit. Call state police first. They'd probably have a better idea."

There's a knock at the door. Green opens it on her way out and points an officer holding a paper bag toward Vasco.

Vasco turns to me. "I can go now, right?"

The officer drops the bag in front of him.

"Not quite. We need to make sure this isn't a wild goose chase you're leading us on."

"Oh, for fuck's sake." Pouting, Vasco grabs the bag and tears it open. Fries spill onto the table as he pulls out the burger, unwraps it, and takes a large bite. "Can I at least get some ketchup for the fries?"

About half an hour later, the Chief and I have set up a small command center in the basement, which is basically my desk and one of the tables from the break area.

"You don't have to stay with me, Chief."

"I'm not driving all the way up to upstate New York tonight." The Chief adjusts his laptop and shuffles several papers. "Plus, there has to be at least two of us to take shifts."

"Shifts?"

"When's the last time you slept?"

Sleep? What's that? "I can hold out until this is over."

"I never said you couldn't. But neither of us is helping anything while our people are in the air and State is trying to coordinate on the ground." He glances at his watch. "By my watch, they still have about an hour until they even land, and then another half hour, at least, until they're ready to mobilize."

"Honestly, Chief, I'm afraid that if I close my eyes, I'll sleep for a week."

He gives me a long look then huffs. "Fine. I'll brew more coffee and you're on food. Anything but pizza." Rising, he heads over to our sad coffee pot.

"I don't know anything but pizza open at this hour."

"Then get me a salad."

I pull up the website, order each of us a salad, then bread sticks, then break down and also order a pizza. My phone buzzes. It's Ben calling.

"Hey, Babe, you should go to bed, I—"

"Sylvy, don't freak out."

"Why would I freak out?" I look over at the Chief to see if he's eavesdropping, but he's got his back to me and is on his cell phone.

Suddenly, the door to the stairwell bursts open and figures in white hazmat suits flood in. "Ben, what's going on?"

"Isabel Winovich just died."

"What?" I look to the Chief. Still on the phone, his face grim, he's walking toward me.

One of the figures is now right in front of me.

"Something happened with her WHISP. They need to isolate you, but I'm coming. Lincoln figured out a more portable system for the measurements. I'll be there soon."

"Be where?" The room is spinning now and I can't catch my breath.

"Detective. You need to come with us."

The Chief appears at my elbow. "It's okay. I'll go with you."

I shake my head. "No. You have to stay here. Keep in touch with the team." I grab my laptop and shove it into its bag."

"Detective."

"I'm coming."

"Sylvy?"

I'd forgotten the cell phone in my hand. I bring it back to my ear. "They're here to take me."

"Okay, I love you. I'll see you soon. I love you."

"I love you, too."

————

IN THE AMBULANCE, I REPEATEDLY TRY TO CONVINCE the three white suits that I feel fine, but apparently the Chief told them I threw up the other day and Ben told them about my unusual WHISP measurements.

"This is just a—"

My molars grind together. "Don't say precaution."

"For your own safety," says the woman starting an IV.

You're fine, right, Liv? "What happened to her?" I think of the other kidnap victims. Help minutes away, and it's probably too late. "Are you sure it was something with her WHISP? How could you know?"

"Just try to relax."

Relaxing is the last thing I want to do, but my eyelids are heavy. I curse my poor sleep, but then I see the IV lady putting a syringe into a sharps container. "What did you give me?" If my arms weren't so heavy, I'd grab her arm.

"Just something to help you sleep."

Bitch. Did I say that aloud?

————

LIV SITS ACROSS FROM ME AT A TABLE SIPPING A

glass of wine. I recognize the outline of my chin, my hair, my ears, and my nose, but the familiarity isn't comforting. Instead, it's a vast, uncanny valley. I want to run, but my limbs won't obey.

You don't like me much, her words are the voice in my head.

"What's to like?" My lips don't move and my limbs don't move, but Liv shrugs her shoulders.

I'm just a part of you.

"But you left me."

She holds out her hands toward me. *You pushed me out.*

"I didn't push you out."

She points to her chest. *You let me go.*

"I didn't know how to keep you in. I would've kept you in. Can you go back in?"

She shakes her head. *It's too late for that.*

"Why are you sick?"

She leans forward. *Something is changing me.*

"What? What's changing you? Can we stop it?"

Something rough is dragging across my forehead. I slit open my eyes. A white suit is leaning over me and stroking my forehead with a gloved hand. Gradually, I see past the glare across the mask to Ben's face.

"That's kinda irritating, actually."

He stops stroking. "Sorry. How are you feeling?"

I swallow a bitter taste. "Fine." Lifting my head, the world tilts and spins. Bile stings the back of my throat. Just the hangover from the sedative, I'm sure. I take a deep breath through my nose and let it out through my mouth. "Except for having been drugged."

"I'm sorry about that."

"Where am I, anyway?"

"Bellevue Hospital."

Not again. "Seriously?"

He shrugs.

"What happened to Isabel?"

"She died."

Right. That part I got. "How? What happened?"

"She started having some seizures, and then her WHISP dispersed and she died."

"It dispersed before she died?"

He nods.

"That's bad, right?"

"We don't know you're affected."

"I know, this is just a precaution." I close my eyes. "How's Lincoln?"

"He's fine. He wanted me to tell you that we have until the end of the month to find a new apartment."

"Funny." *Don't scare me.* I open my eyes. "Wait, what time is it? How did the raid go? Did they find the kidnap victims?"

"We're still waiting to hear."

I stare at him, eyes wide. "Well, get me my laptop or a radio or something."

"Sylvy."

"I'm serious, Ben. And maybe you should go."

Hurt flashes in his eyes. "You want me to go?"

"If those people are alive, they're infected. You and Lincoln, the lab, my measurements, may be their only hope."

"You're serious. Sylvy, I'm a particle physicist, not a doctor."

"And this is a particle disease. You're smart, Lincoln's smart, you'll figure out something. Take my measurements and go figure something out."

Doubt replaces the hurt.

"You can do this, Babe. You may be *my* only hope, too."

CHAPTER 24

Excerpt from Transcript of Session 52:
Dr. Aziz Fritz with Det. S. Harbinger

Fritz: Can I ask you about your faith?
Harbinger: Okay. I don't have much of one. My mom was
Lutheran and my dad was Episcopal. My aunt was Catholic and
tried to get me to go to catechism after my parents were killed,
but I wouldn't go.
Fritz: Is Ben religious?
Harbinger: No. He's agnostic. Why?
Fritz: I was just wondering if you thought a higher power had a
hand in what happened.
Harbinger: Do you really think I, of all people, would have an
"everything happens for a reason" philosophy on life?
Fritz: That's not the motto of all religions.
Harbinger: Technically, no. I guess I'm just not that spiritual.

WHEN I FINALLY GET MY LAPTOP AND PHONE, I
immediately text the Chief.

Harbinger: What's going on?

Chief: Everything in place. Watching.

Harbinger: Time? What's it look like?

Chief: Looks like house. I knw kidnapping, but circmsts. WHISP danger. You knw bigger than kn.

Harbinger: Can I get vid?

Chief: Will patch thru.

I grab my laptop, rip off its plastic biohazard bag and fire it up. The battery is almost dead.

"I need a plug!" I try to get out of bed and alarms blare from assorted machines as white suits come running.

"I need a sedative!" shouts one of the suits.

"You do not need a sedative." I get back in bed. "Look, I'm fine." I hold up the laptop cord. "I just need to plug in my laptop."

"You really should be resting, Detective."

"I promise to lie very still while I watch my laptop, and I promise to need a sedative if I don't get my laptop plugged in."

The woman who called for sedatives considers the options long enough that I think she's going to just sedate me again, but finally she shakes her head and rolls her eyes. "Just plug it in."

The man next to her grabs the computer's cord and finds an empty slot in a power strip.

"Thanks, um, doctor…?"

"Doctor Carter. Don't thank me. Any added stress will probably hasten your condition. I don't want another death on my watch, but you're a cop, so you'd probably be stressed in your sleep, anyway."

I nod. "Probably."

She turns.

"Wait."

She turns back with a sigh. "Yes?"

"Another death? Were you treating Isabel?"

She nods.

"What happened to her?" I've already heard it from Ben, but I want a first-hand account.

"We'll know more after the autopsy."

"Did she say anything?"

"She wasn't coherent at the end. She'd had several massive seizures."

Poor Isabel. "Seizures?"

"Yes, about a quarter of an hour before she died, she began having intermittent grand mal seizures."

"And did her WHISP really dissipate *before* she died?"

Dr. Carter clears her throat and tries to cross her arms, but the suit prevents it. "It appeared to, yes."

"Maybe…"

"Maybe what?"

"Maybe you could get a Faraday cage in here. Put it around me. Maybe it would help keep my WHISP together." *Keep it together, Liv.* "Couldn't hurt, right?"

"Hmmm. I'll see what I can do." She walks away before I can say more.

I'm not sure if she's just humoring me, but in truth, I might just be humoring myself, so I don't press the issue. Instead, I turn to my laptop, login, and find the link the Chief sent me. It's a bad wifi connection, probably because I'm deep in the bowels of a hospital, and the signal keeps cutting out, but when it's clear, I see exactly what the Chief said, a house. The house looks like a modest, two-story farmhouse. There's also a dilapidated barn. Other than a porch light, there aren't any other lights on at the house or any light coming from the barn. I don't see any activity and there aren't any cars visible. Maybe I've seen too many movies, but I text the Chief.

Harbinger: Bet it's under barn.

Chief: Yes. Will check barn. Smiley emoji.

I want to text Ben, but I also don't want to bother him. He was wearing his Ben-lost-in-physics face when he left here with my latest WHISP measurements. *You're fine, right Liv? Feelin' good?* I close my eyes and send out what I think is a wave of upbeat, healthy vibes. My stomach lurches and I bite back bile. Not a good omen. Hopefully, it's only a bit of nausea left over from being drugged. *Please let it be that.* I focus instead on the screen. Nothing happens for a minute, then five, then close to ten minutes later, I see a shadow dart behind the barn. Moments later, it's followed by several more shadows. *Here we go.* Please let us not be too late. Did Isabel ever reconcile with her husband or other relatives before she died? It's possible the other kidnap victims will never get the chance. But then, I remember Latrina's brother. Maybe it's better that way.

I can't see anything else for now. My mind drifts to Lincoln and how much I must have hurt him before I got Liv. I'd like to think I wasn't as bad as Latrina's brother, but only by degrees, and it wasn't like I was mother of the year before that. *Wait a second. Are these regretful deathbed thoughts?* Okay. Let's just try to be a better me from now on. I sit up straighter in the bed and spend several minutes adjusting pillows to get comfortable again, all the while keeping a hawk eye on my laptop. *Why are hospital beds the most uncomfortable things in the world?* You would think comfort would go hand-in-hand with healing. The video feed blacks out completely. I grab my phone.

Harbinger: Talk to me. Feeds dead.

Chief: Found a trap door in barn. No heat sigs in house, so going in.

I hold my breath. *Please, dear lord, let this not be a shit-show.*

Chief: New feed. https://nypd/ops/swat/helmet2

I type the new feed into my computer and fat finger it twice in my haste. *Come on!* On the third try the screen comes to life again, but is frozen on a shot of a bright light shining into a dark shaft with a metal ladder on one side. I refresh and I'm staring at the wall of the shaft, but not the one with the ladder. The next refresh shows the barrel of an assault rifle and a dimly lit corridor. I punch the refresh again and again, maddened by the sluggish results: more corridor, a room of glass that looks like a laboratory, armed men in dark clothing spilling around a corner, a flash of light, then nothing but blackness. Refresh. Refresh. Refresh.

Harbinger: Chief?

Chief: Mines out too. Shot camera.

Harbinger: Audio?

Chief: Gunfire.

I tear off a hunk of my thumbnail before I even realize I've been chewing it. *Please. Please. Please.*

Chief: Eyes on kn victims.

Harbinger: Alive?

Chief: Y, some

Chief: more than 4

Chief: Green calling.

More than four? Did they hit a shelter in another city and we just missed it? Or maybe they were pulling WHISPers off the streets before they got tired of only getting one at a time.

"Detective?"

I jump roughly a foot off the bed before I realize it's only Dr. Carter and a small army of other white suits. "Yeah?"

"These gentlemen and ladies are from the university. They're here to construct you a Faraday cage."

"Oh. Right." I can't believe she got one for me. "Okay."

The other white suits start unpacking boxes of copper wires and pvc pipes. One, a guy with more piercings than I can count, glances at my laptop and phone. "They won't work in there, you know."

"Yeah. I know." I forgot, but I knew that. Since the feed for the laptop is already down, I shut it and concentrate on getting out a few last texts.

Sylvy: Going dark. Asked for Faraday cage.

After about a minute. Ben: Clever girl. Xoxo

Sylvy: xoxo

Harbinger: Going dark. Part of treatment.

Chief: ??? Kk will come see you when I can. Or call? Speaker phn?

Harbinger: Good idea. Thnx.

Sylvia: Hey Buddy, didn't want to bug ya, but your dad probably told you I'm going dark for a bit. You can still call, but I know you're busy, so don't break for me. Kiss kiss.

After about two minutes. Lincoln: Complications, but may be onto something. Hold tight. Heart emoji.

Broken heart emoji. Broken heart emoji. Broken heart emoji. Such a good kid. He deserves better. Sigh. *Now, what did we say about that kind of talk?* I hold out the phone. "Can someone take this for me? I might get a call soon. You can put it on speaker."

"Um..." A white suit from the university pauses in tightening a bolt and tries to touch the screen through his gloves. "Sorry, won't work. Better give 'em your land line here."

"Crap." I reach for the ancient manila device and text the number to the Chief, then to Lincoln, then Ben.

"Detective?"

"Dr. Carter?"

"We'd like to do a final blood draw before they encapsulate you."

"Fine, okay, yeah." I stick out my arm for the vampire with the needle and barely feel her draining me. "Um, I should probably use the facilities, too."

Dr. Carter's sculpted eyebrows knit neatly together in a dishwater blonde forehead scarf and the corners of her mouth turn down. "You do understand that you could die at any time, and you have a bedpan."

"You said Isabel had a seizure first, right?"

A grudging nod.

"Well, then I think I might have a minute to pee."

With a slight head shake that doesn't move her mask, she turns to another white suit. "Ann Marie, will you please disconnect Detective Harbinger and take her to the restroom."

"Of course, doctor."

It takes considerably longer than expected to extract me from my various monitors and whatnot. The worst of which are the leads on my scalp to monitor my brain. Those wires go through a kind of circuit board box that has to weigh close to ten pounds and hangs off a lanyard around my neck. Fortunately, the bathroom isn't far; otherwise, I might've gotten whiplash from the thing swinging back and forth. After I use the facilities, I try to get a less clinical description of Isabel's demise from Ann Marie.

"So, did you take care of the other lady, too—Isabel?"

Ann Marie nods. "She was a sweet lady. That was very sad."

"Did she say anything? I mean, just before."

"She was kind of rambling. A lot of nonsense. She mentioned Yosef and Yonny, which I guess were her friends. She kept saying 'Don't leave me' even when I held her hand."

"Did her husband come to visit her?"

"No, but I think she may have spoken to him on the phone."

I hope it was a good talk. "Oh. Good?"

"Well, she was crying afterwards, but I couldn't tell if they were, you know, happy tears."

Probably not. Halfway back to the bed, the room tilts and I grab for the railing on the wall.

Ann Marie's hand is under my arm at the shoulder. "Are you okay?"

The dizziness passes. "Yeah. Yeah. Probably just forgot to eat again."

She smiles through her mask. "Sometimes I set an alarm on my phone to remind me to eat. Do you carry little snack bags with you? As a police officer, I know you don't always have time to make a lunch, but carrot sticks and peanut butter crackers can go a long way."

I'm about to tell her about the power bars, but they taste bad enough that I rarely eat them. "Thanks. I'll try that."

Back at the bed, Ann Marie begins the lengthy process of reconnecting me. "Did Isabel show any other symptoms besides the seizures?"

"Well," Ann Marie hesitates a beat, "she did say she was a little light-headed."

Oh crap.

"Listen, let me bring you something to eat. How 'bout I get you some Jello?"

Okay, Mom. "Sure, that'd be great."

After I'm reconnected, the troop from "the university" bolts the pieces of the cage together, having slid the bottom section under my bed while I was in the bathroom. It's larger than I thought it'd be, encompassing the entire bed and one of the bedside cabinets. Still, my throat tightens as they ratchet the last bolt and my breaths come fast and shallow.

"Um, question. How am I supposed to get out of here? It doesn't look like there's a door to this thing."

The white suit in front of me turns to the one beside him. "She has a point, Ahmen."

"In an emergency, the easiest exit would be with wire cutters, but this panel here"— Ahmen points to the foot of the bed—"has only two bolts."

My escape hatch is small and shrinking every moment I stare at it. "Okay. Thanks. Did you by chance bring wire cutters?"

The other man shakes his head.

"Ah, well, no worries, I'm sure the hospital has some handy."

If either of them picked up on my sarcasm, they're hiding it well.

Sigh. "No, really, thanks for getting this together on such short notice."

"I hope it helps."

Me too.

CHAPTER 25

Excerpt from Transcript of Session 16:
Dr. Aziz Fritz with Det. S. Harbinger

Harbinger: I just don't see where any of this is going.
Fritz: Our sessions specifically or therapy in general?
Harbinger: Therapy in general. It's not like it's going to change anything.
Fritz: You're right, therapy doesn't often change a person's situation. It's designed to make that situation more bearable to the individual. To give individuals an outlet or skills to better cope with their situation.
Harbinger: It's all just talk though, isn't it? And what if there is no way to cope? What if there shouldn't be a way to cope? What if the situation is too fucked up to cope, but you still can't change it? What then?
Fritz: The human mind will always find a way to cope with a situation. The question is whether or not that way is healthy for the individual.

AS I WAIT IN MY COPPER PRISON FOR THE PHONE TO ring, a growing unease blossoms in my belly. The saying is 'bad news travels fast,' and that's often true, but I expected good news to travel fast, too, in this case: Yes, we saved the kidnap victims; yes, we busted the bad guys. The silence is deafening. Silence means complications, and in police work, complications usually mean deaths. Trapped in my little cage, all I can do is toss and turn in a fruitless bid to find a position that doesn't make my body cringe with discomfort. It's been less than an hour, but every second feels like its own lifetime, and I'm regretting my earlier "flash of brilliance" of suggesting the cage, but Ben seemed to think it was a good idea, too.

"Detective?"

I stop twisting the sheet and peer through the wire. It's Ann Marie. "Hello again."

She proffers a Styrofoam cup too big to fit through the gaps in the wires. "Here's the Jello I promised." She examines the wire cage more closely. "Oh, um, I guess I could feed you through the wires."

I'm about to decline when my stomach erupts in protests. "Ah, sure. Maybe just hand me the spoon through the gaps."

"Yes. That should work." She peels off a cling wrap cover, fills the spoon with a jiggling, red chunk, and then slides it through one of the openings.

As I take the first bite, my mouth waters. Who knew hospital Jello could be this good? Eager for a second, I slide the spoon back to her. We repeat the process a few times with great success before one large globule ends up splatting on the floor.

"Oh shoot." Ann Marie grabs some paper towels from the dispenser and cleans the mess then scrutinizes the cage again. "I've got some cookies, too, but I'd have to break them in half, at least, I think. Oh, but carrot sticks will go right through, and apple slices."

"Any of those are probably better than the Jello." I smile.

"I'll go see what I can—"

The room telephone jangles to life and my heart stops briefly. "Can you answer that for me, please?"

Ann Marie nods, picks up the receiver, and holds it up to the cage wires for me, but when she touches the phone to the wires, a burst of static assaults my ears.

"Hold it a little further from the wire, please."

Ann Marie backs it off an inch.

"Chief?"

"Harbing—." Buzz. Buzz. "—victims" Buzz. "—need."

I motion Ann Marie to back up a little more. "Sorry, Chief. I'm in a Faraday cage. I didn't catch that." But now, even with my hand cupped around my ear, the phone is too far away to hear him. "Ann Marie, can you just relay the message for me?"

She nods and puts the receiver to her ear. "I'll try." She stares ahead for a few seconds and nods to herself, then turns to me. "He says the compound is state-of-the-art, and that they took some heavy casualties in SWAT, from an armed response, but that it might've been worse if they hadn't surprised them." She stops and listens once again. "He says they found the victims, but they're afraid to move them? Um, something about their WHISPs being unstable? He says that Ben thinks you might be able to help somehow. That he thinks your inoculation was diluted? Does that make sense to you?"

Maybe? I nod.

"He says, Ben is trying to get you released from quarantine right now to get you to the compound. Lincoln is already the—"

"Wait! Lincoln is there?" What is Lincoln doing at the heart of this bioweapon?

She nods. "He's trying to make sense of the records they were able to recover, but many were wiped as SWAT came in. Some kind of fail-safe? And that CompUServer Plus is there trying to recover the data, too."

Green and Beaulieu must have their hands full. I'm still

stunned that Lincoln is there, but if Ben is here, there's no sense in chewing out the Chief through Ann Marie when I can chew Ben out in person.

"He says you have to hurry, so he's going to hang up now. Um, thank you, sir."

"Ann Marie, you have to help get me out of here."

She nods. "Okay, how do I do that?"

"They left the ratchet for the bolts over there." I point to a cabinet with a countertop then crawl to the foot of my bed. "And this panel only has two bolts."

After retrieving the ratchet, she returns and begins loosening the bolts. "But I thought you needed to stay in here."

So did I. "Guess not."

Working the bolt as fast as she can manage, I wish I could do something to help. Then I remember I'm in a hospital gown, and been there, done that. I start opening the drawers of the one bedside table in the cage with me. "Hey, Ann Marie, do you know where my clothes are?"

She shrugs. "Sorry. Doctor Carter would know."

The room is empty except for Anne Marie and me, so I find the call button and press it once, then two more times for good measure.

After an agonizing few minutes, another white suit reenters the room. When it gets closer, I spot Dr. Carter's scowl on the other side of the faceplate.

"Yes, Detective?" Then she sees what Ann Marie is doing. "Nurse Fascing, stop that right now. What's going on here?"

Ann Marie pauses her ratcheting.

"What's going on here is, I need to get out of this cage and I need my clothes. Haven't they told you yet?"

"Someone tried to authorize your release from the quarantine, but I overrode it. Now lie back."

"What! You don't understand. There are lives at stake and I might be able to help them."

"And you might not, and kill yourself in the process. Now, you asked me for this cage and I provided it. You're safe in there and can't infect anyone else."

Suddenly, I see an ugly gleam in Dr. Carter's eye that I hadn't noticed before. "Is that what you're afraid of? It's not like I want out to go traipsing through the city. NYPD is taking me to an isolated location in Upstate New York. The only people I could possibly infect there are already infected." *Except Lincoln.* I swallow hard.

Dr. Carter looks at my hand and I realize I'm gripping the wire so tight, my finger is bleeding.

"Please lie back. Don't make me sedate you again, Detective."

I'm about to tell her to come in and get me, but then I see my IV bag hanging on the other side of the wire. I could rip it out, but they'd probably just get a syringe on a stick like they do with rabid dogs. Like molasses in my brain, it dawns on me. I'm screwed. Not only that, but I'm imprisoned in a cage I actually asked for. That's what really stings. "I need to call the Chief."

"You need to rest, Detective. Nurse, I believe your shift is just about over, isn't it?"

"Yes, Dr. Carter."

"Right. Then you have some paperwork to complete, don't you?"

"Of course, Dr. Carter." With a pained look of sympathy aimed at me, Ann Marie shuffles away.

"Please try to get some rest, Detective. I'll let you know if anything changes." Dr. Carter turns away.

My mind is doing laps around my skull. Does she really outrank the NYPD? She might if she's a part of the city public health machine and definitely would if she's part of the CDC. I never thought to ask exactly who the ones in the white suits were. But surely, if there's a chance Ben has found a way I can help those other infected people, they'd have to let me do it, right?

Another cold thought leeches into my head. Maybe not. Maybe they'd rather just contain this and let us all die, then the problem dies with us, right? *No, no, no. Get a grip, Sylvy, not everything is a conspiracy.* Even if the Upstate New York lab is the only terrorist compound working on this specific bioweapon, there could be others, right? A cure or treatment or whatever now, when only a handful of us are infected, is much better than the alternative.

I'm sure Ben's request just got blocked because he didn't have any authority behind it. The Chief will find some authority and then I'll be out and on my way. But, dammit, how long will that take?

I'm fidgeting in the bed again, trying to straighten my hospital gown and tie it better, just in case, when I hear the scrape of metal on metal and a glint of silver catches my eye. *Oh Ann Marie, you clever girl you.* She's left the ratchet at the end of the bed, sticking through the wires. The bolts for the smallest panel are on the outside, but one of the larger panels has bolts on the inside. Pantomiming stretching out on the bed in case Dr. Carter isn't as interested in the charts she's perusing as she appears, I grasp hold of the metal handle while keeping my eyes on her and another white suit that just entered the room. I'm positive this plan is insane since not only will I have to get myself out of the cage without anybody seeing me and then bulrush the door, but also because I'm sure there's a staging area outside the door and then guards on the other side of that. Oh well, can't blame a gal for trying. Wouldn't be the first time I've broken out of this hospital, though last time I never would've made it without Ben.

The ratchet head gets stuck between the wires. *Crap.* I sit up in front of it with my legs crossed and fold my arms behind me. Hopefully, if anyone notices me, they'll think I'm meditating. Twisting the tool gently back and forth, I feel it starting to slide through when one of the white suits approaches the cage. My heart leaps into my mouth. As they get closer, I see it's not Dr. Carter. I don't think I've seen this man before.

"Hi. I'm taking over for Ann Marie. She said she was going to get you some cookies or carrot sticks or something?"

"Haha, yeah. That's okay, I'm not really hungry anymore." My stomach growls, but I'm not sure he hears it in his suit.

"It's no trouble."

"No really, I'm fine. I just want to, um, meditate." Meditate? Really? When did I get to be such a horrible liar? *Calm yourself, Harbinger.*

"Alrighty. Just let me know if you need anything. My name's Sundar, but you can call me Sunny."

"Sure. Thanks."

He turns his back and walks over toward Dr. Carter at her temporary desk. She should be going off shift soon, too, shouldn't she? Unless she's anything like me. I wiggle the tool more vigorously now that they both are turned away, but the angle's wrong. I shift and pain stabs into my back like a flechette. Biting my tongue to keep from crying out, I glance behind me and almost shout again. *What. The. Hell.* Liv is pressed up against the cage and contorted out of her normal place behind me. Also, her silhouette is not lining up with me like a shadow, but has its hands up and pressed against the copper wires. I choke on my own spit as the hollow shock of wrongness pulses through me. It's hurting her...us.

Leaning forward, I twist to get her away from the wires then check to see if anyone else saw what just happened. Fortunately, Dr. Carter and Sunny are ignoring me. *I'm sorry, Liv.* The pain and pressure is gone, but in its place is a general twitchiness and discomfort. Suddenly, it's as if the cage is electrified and I'm afraid to touch it. I've got to get out of here. *Fuck it.*

Blatantly now, I grab the ratchet and yank it through the wire with one mighty jerk of the wrist.

"Hey! What are you doing?" Dr. Carter is storming over.

Oh crap. I drop the ratchet into the blankets. "My sheet was caught."

She holds out her hand. "Give it to me."

Shit. I hold up my empty hands. "What?"

"You know what. The ratchet."

I'm debating how to proceed when the door bursts open and Ben storms in like a knight in shining armor, wielding bolt cutters instead of a sword.

CHAPTER 26

Excerpt from Transcript of Session 11:
Dr. Aziz Fritz with Det. S. Harbinger

Harbinger: I'm finding it hard to love my son. How messed up is that?

Fritz: I don't think it is messed up, at all. Many parents have strained relationships with their children.

Harbinger: Yeah, but that's when their kid is a murderer or druggie or kleptomaniac or drop out or something. Lincoln's a great kid. Any parent's dream: smart, funny, caring, never been in trouble with the law. Any other mom would love the shit out of that kid. It's not even like it's his fault.

Fritz: It being his WHISP.

Harbinger: [Nods] And I don't even know why Ben is still with me. How could you stay with someone who didn't love their own kid?

Fritz: I'm sure he knows that you still love Lincoln even if it's difficult right now.

Harbinger: What if it never gets any easier?

DR. CARTER WHIRLS AROUND AND SUNNY, WHO HAD

plopped down on a chair by the door, springs into action by standing.

"What's the meaning of this? You are breaking a secure quarantine area and endangering the life of my patient! Sundar, call security!"

Ben strides past a frozen Sunny to my cage and holds up a card on a lanyard around his neck. "Multipass."

A punch-drunk giggle escapes my throat.

Dr. Carter is flummoxed. "What?"

"And I've got one for Mrs. Corban Dallas, as well."

"What the hell are you—"

"It's from a movie." One of my favorites. "He means to say he got the proper clearance to override you and we're outta here."

Ben shoves a piece of paper in her face and attacks the cage with the bolt cutters.

"You know, I was just about to bust out of here myself, right?" I hold up the ratchet.

Ben grunts as he snaps through wires. "I know you were, but you need to save your energy."

Wait. "Where did you get bolt cutters?"

Snap. Snip. Snap. "A sweet woman nurse heard me say your name and asked if I was coming to get you out. She was very helpful in finding a maintenance closet with bolt cutters."

Guess the hospital did have those lying around. "Aw, good ole Ann Marie."

"Wow, they got this put together fast, didn't they?"

"Yep." I peer around Ben. Dr. Carter is now on the phone and Sunny is still standing around looking useless. "Hey, Sunny. Can you get me my clothes, please?"

"What?"

"My clothes. Can I have them, please?"

As he ferrets around the room looking, I turn back to Ben. He's got about half of an exit hole snipped. "Well, I thought about how Isabel's WHISP dissipated before she died and thought it might help keep Li—mine together."

"Right." He pauses while his mind whirrs.

"Hey, hello. Doesn't matter now. We gotta go."

His eyes refocus. "Right, sorry."

Sunny approaches the cage, but his arms are empty.

"Sunny?"

"Couldn't find them."

You've got to be kidding me. "Can you find someone who might know what happened to them, please?"

He nods dumbly and wanders off.

I'm not holding my breath. "Hey, Babe, you didn't happen to bring me some extra clothes, did you?"

Ben catches my eye. "Um..."

I shake my head. Not again.

———

BUT SURPRISINGLY, SUNNY COMES THROUGH, IN A manner of speaking. He comes back just as Ben is helping me crawl through the hole he's cut in the cage. Distracted by a scraping pain across my back that I'm sure is the wire tips snagging in my skin, it doesn't register that what he has in his hands isn't my grey pants and blazer.

"Ow! Am I bleeding?"

"What? Where?" Ben looks me over.

"My back. I think the wires hooked me."

Confusion muddles Ben's face. "Sylvy, your back didn't come anywhere near the wires." Then panic. "Oh God, are you feeling okay?"

Must've been Liv again. I swallow hard. "No, no, I'm fine. Let's go. Just let me get dressed."

Sunny hands me a set of scrubs and a pair of grippy, hospital socks. "It's all I could find."

I think it's odd that he and Dr. Carter are still wearing their hazmat suits. "No, that's great, Sunny, thanks. It's better than the gown."

I pull up the pants under the gown and then turn modestly away and tear it up over my head before donning the scrub shirt. Tossing the gown on the floor, I grab Ben's shoulder for support and slide the socks onto my feet. When I lift my head, the room spins and I get a mouthful of bile. He steadies me as I teeter.

"Hey, whoa, Sylvy, what's going on? You're not fine."

I swallow the bitter stomach fluid. "No, it's fine. I just whipped my head up too quick and I haven't eaten much and I was sedated earlier. I'm fine."

"Maybe we better—"

"I said, I'm fine. You said I could help. Let's go."

Dr. Carter, now off the phone, presides over us, her smug face practically glowing under her suit's mask. "I told you, you were endangering her life. You should've left her in the cage."

My fist clenches, but then her words trigger a thought. "Ben. Are we sure we can get me out of here without running into any other WHISPers?"

He smiles. "Don't you worry. NYPD is on it. They've blocked off a route for us and there's a chopper waiting on the roof."

"Whoa. When did we enter a spy movie?"

Concern returns to his face. "You're sure you're okay?"

I nod, but not too fast. "Let's do this."

———

HAVING FLOWN IN A HELICOPTER BEFORE, I KNEW IT was nauseating, but this time it's all I can do to not technicolor yawn all over my husband's lap. To his credit, probably seeing my green gills, he doesn't try to talk to me. Best I don't open my mouth. But I'm not worried. Not really. Not exactly. No one mentioned nausea or vomiting with Isabel, just the seizures, and since getting out of that cage, I haven't felt any additional twinges from Liv. The pilot's voice crackles over our headphones.

"Two minutes."

Two more minutes. I can do two minutes.

"Sylvy. Lincoln knows you're coming, so don't worry. We have him isolated."

I nod and take a deep breath. "How is this going to work?"

"I'm going to use an amplifier to send certain pulses through Li— through your WHISP. We're then going to check the way the particles react to those pulses and see if we can find a frequency where they reflect them back."

Another deep breath, in through the nose and out through the mouth. "How does that help?"

"We think the WHISP bug is sort of like a prion, coming into contact with the particles in a WHISP and changing them, their properties and their behaviors. The delay in causing death to the person is that there has to be a relay between the brain's electrical signaling that amplifies the modifications in the WHISP instead of the brain signals re-exerting control over the WHISP's properties and behavior. If we can get the WHISP to start reflecting a new non-damaging relay, then maybe we can stop the original bug's relay." He stops to breathe. "Does that make any sense?"

Nope. I nod. But something he said did stick. "A new non-damaging relay? How do you know if a relay or signal or whatever will or won't cause damage?"

His gaze flits away then back. "We have some theories. Your WHISP was definitely exposed to Isabel's infected WHISP, but either you're somehow immune to the WHISP bug or..."

The helicopter takes a sharp turn, begins its descent, and

leaves my stomach about twenty feet above our heads. "Ah." My throat burns. "Or what?"

"Or the bug's relay is developing more slowly with you for whatever reason."

"But why do you need me? What about the other victims that're still alive? Why not test them?"

The pilot's voice comes over the speakers again, "Touching down."

We unstrap and take off our headsets, then Ben gets out first and helps me out. Soon, we're doing that super-authentic crouch-run away from the helicopter toward the old barn, which is now lit up nearly as bright as day with giant spotlights. I spy the Chief standing in the doorway and we head for him as the helicopter takes off again.

"Harbinger, Ben, glad you made it in okay."

Behind him, I see a three-by-six-foot rectangular hole in the floor of the barn surrounded by smaller, yet still blinding, lights. Behind me, a siren sounds and I turn my head to see an ambulance pull away at speed. "What's the situation?"

"We took some casualties, like I said. There was a significant armed response here, but surprise was our friend. I think everyone's going to make it, but two deaths on the other side. No ID's yet and the ten we have in custody aren't saying a word, not the scientists or the guards. My guess is this is part of something much larger."

I nod. "Well, we kinda knew that already from all the levels taken to hide what was going on. What about the victims?"

The Chief's gaze flicks to Ben then back to me. "So, this is more complicated. They're in a secure room made of glass. A SWAT member who used to be on the bomb squad didn't like the look right from the get go and he was right. The door's rigged with explosives. We're looking for an alternative, or way to diffuse, but right now we're in a holding pattern."

"But they're alive?"

"Not all of them, but we're trying to identify the other five and find out where they came from."

"Can we not communicate with them through the glass?"

He shakes his head and Ben takes over. "It looks like the ones still alive are all sedated. They're strapped in and have IV drips. My guess is they were doing more testing on the WHISP bug here, maybe trying to make it more virulent, or faster acting, or longer range." He stops and shakes his head. "Anyway, that doesn't matter. Let's get you inside."

Until he said something, the cold was like a faint prickle on my bare face and arms, barely registering, but now a chill chomps down with icicle teeth into my spine and shivers clack my teeth together. "G-good idea. You c-coming, Chief?"

"Not right now. I'm headed for the house. They went into town for pizza and should be back soon."

At the mention of pizza, my mouth is fairly dripping, but food can wait. "B-bring some when you come." I approach the trapdoor and study the hole and the ladder. A SWAT member is standing guard both at the top and bottom and the one at the bottom is talking to a state police trooper. The SWAT member at the top nods to Ben. As I get on hands and knees to back down onto the ladder, he calls out, "Two coming down."

The metal rungs are cold enough to hurt my hands, so I climb down as quickly as I can. Once at the bottom, I blow on my hands and rub them together to restore circulation.

"Detective Harbinger?"

I look at the face of the bottom SWAT guy more closely. "Schmitty?"

"Yeah, hah, um, everything okay?"

Not even a little. But I'm slightly better than last time he saw me, running barefoot through a WHISP protest in a hospital gown. At least now, I have socks on. "Sure. So, you joined SWAT?"

"Is it that obvious?" Smiling he lifts his assault rifle.

Statistics give a ten percent mortality rate within the first two years, but I try to smile back.

Ben reaches the ground and Schmitty's smile regresses as he recognizes him, too, but Schmitty nods politely. Ben points down the left branch of the hallway. "This way."

"Lookin' good. Take care of yourself." I give Schmitty a thumbs-up before following Ben down the corridor. It isn't much warmer down here, but at least it isn't windy. As we walk, I notice a fair number of bullet ricochets and blood spatter on the walls along with a few drying pools on the polished concrete floor. The assault really was a blood bath. A wave of uncharacteristic queasiness rushes over me and I put a hand to my forehead and find it wet with sweat. I'm still cold. Not good. I wipe the sweat away and breathe through my mouth. *Keep it together, Sylvy.* After the murder of Yosef, I expected violence, but I wasn't expecting this much security. Along with the explosive-rigged door, the scale of the operation makes me very nervous.

"Hey, I know the SWAT, bomb-squad guy is probably working on that door, but did they check this whole building out for booby-traps?"

"I think so."

Not comforting. We reach an open door and enter a lab with equipment similar to what I've seen in Ben's lab only bigger, shinier, and more. The copper cage in the corner makes me flinch, but that's probably where I'm headed anyway, so I start toward it.

Ben grabs my wrist. "No, not this time." He points to a chair in the middle of the room with leather arm and leg straps and a science-fictionesque helmet with wires coming out of it.

"You're kidding."

"Nope. I won't strap you in, but that's where you need to sit." He rubs the back of my hand and frowns. "Your hand is like ice."

Slipping it out of his grip, I turn away and walk to the chair before he notices the sweat on my forehead. "Those ladder rungs were really cold." I sit. I thought the chair was metal, but it's actually plastic. Probably has something to do with conductivity. Glancing behind me, I see there's an area for Liv with a clear, plastic barrier around it. It doesn't hurt when she slips inside, but I don't like the way she looks trapped in a bubble.

Ben comes over and lowers the helmet onto my head, adjusting it until it's snug.

"I thought you were going to be bombarding Liv with the waves or whatever."

"I am. This is to see your brain's reaction, if any, to the different frequencies."

"Ah. How did you even know that's what this thing's for?"

He clears his throat and doesn't meet my eye.

I get it. He and Lincoln have probably been designing something similar for when their testing gets approved. "Oh."

He moves over to a computer terminal next to the machine. "Okay. I'm going to start slow with a relatively normal radio frequency that you should come into contact with daily. I'll increase or decrease it very slowly. Let me know if you feel anything, even if it seems like it's nothing or just a scalp itch. Let me know, okay?"

"Okay."

He lets out a breath and I close my eyes.

"Here we—"

"Ben!"

CHAPTER 27

Excerpt from Transcript of Session 41:
Dr. Aziz Fritz with Det. S. Harbinger

Fritz: So it never occurred to you that climbing into a particle accelerator might create a WHISP?
Harbinger: I wasn't really thinking about myself at the time. Ben was bleeding out, Lincoln was in danger, and it was the only thing I could think of to save them.
Fritz: Are you sorry you did it?
Harbinger: What kind of question is that? Of course not.
Fritz: So, you could say that your WHISP is the price for saving the lives of your husband and son.
Harbinger: I suppose you could put it that way.
Fritz: Then why is it something bad? Why isn't your WHISP a positive reminder of your sacrifice for your family?
Harbinger: [Shrugs] I just don't see that way.

MY HEART POUNDS PAINFULLY AGAINST MY STERNUM and my eyes fly open. One of Ben's coworkers is standing in the doorway. It might even be Naomi. Her red-brown hair is pulled back into a messy ponytail and her lab coat is open showing jeans and a stained sweatshirt. She looks about fifteen, which means she's in her mid-twenties. Lincoln's age.

"Naomi, I'm just about to start trying some waves on—"

"Something's happening. Some victims have started to have seizures, I think we might be too late."

His face falls like a glass shattering on the floor. My chest tightens and crushes my heart. *Dammit. Why did we stop to talk to the Chief? What was I thinking?*

"Ben."

He's still staring at Naomi. "Well, how are they on the door?"

"Jackson thinks he's close to a temporary disarm."

Temporary disarm. *What does that even mean?* "Wait, we can't zap them through the glass?"

Ben finally looks at me and shakes his head. "The glass will disrupt the wave. How long did Isabel last when she started having seizures?"

I try to shake my head, but can't with the helmet on. "Not long. Ten minutes, maybe fifteen." Really, I'm just trying to be hopeful. I don't even think it was that long.

He turns back to Naomi. "They just started seizing?"

She nods.

"Ben, we can still do this. Just don't go slow and don't start slow. I'm sure you've looked at my WHISP measurements and calculated a probable frequency or whatever. Just start there."

He shakes his head. "No. Sylvy, I could kill you."

"You kill me, this WHISP bug thing kills me, what's the difference?"

"You could be immune!"

"We both know that's highly unlikely. Now come on. Us doing nothing isn't helping anyone."

He shakes his head, but moves to the screen. "I'm still going to start slow, but I'll increase faster. Let me know—"

"If I feel anything, yeah, got it. Let's do this."

"Naomi, go back and monitor the others. Send a runner if there are any changes. Get readings, if you can, when they get the door open."

"Okay." She tears off down the hallway.

He looks into my eyes. "I'm starting. I love you."

"I love you, too. Do it."

And I feel nothing. Good. But after a few seconds, one of my ears starts ringing. I don't mention it. It's annoying, not life threatening.

"You okay? Talk to me, Sylvy."

"I'm fine. I don't feel anything." *Do you, Liv?* I want to look at her, but I can't turn my head in the helmet, so I try to picture her behind me in the bubble of plastic.

"I'm increasing it now."

The other ear starts ringing. It's nothing. Not even as bad as a rock concert. I imagine Liv vibrating. Ben said radio waves, right? Maybe she's dancing. Pain slices up my spine and enters the back of my skull splitting my brain in half. I must be screaming, but I can't hear anything but the ringing in my ears. Then everything is dark and quiet. Gradually, light seeps in and Liv is there in front of me.

This isn't going to work. As her voice sounds in my head, she shakes hers slowly.

"But we have to save those people, we have to save us."

We were never infected.

"But the measurements."

They're off for a different reason.

"So, I'm not partially infected? There's nothing we can do to help them?"

She turns her head away from me. *Maybe there is.*

"What?"

We know what Ben is trying to do. If we go in there, maybe we can do it ourselves.

I only have a very vague comprehension of what Ben was trying to do, but she must know that already. "And if we can't?"

She makes the gesture of an explosion with her hands. *Poof.* The light dims. "Wait!"

But first you have to tell Ben to stop. He has to stop or he's going to kill us.

All is darkness and silence again. Then there's buzzing in my ears and someone is shoving daggers into my brain. "S-stop," I whisper. Nothing happens. "Stop!" Sweet relief. My body sags and my head slips out of the helmet.

"Sylvy! God! Sylvy! Are you okay?" Ben is there, his arms around me, holding me up. "Oh, God. Talk to me. What have I done? Oh, sweetheart. Talk to me, Baby. Talk to me."

"It's okay. I'm okay."

"No, you're not. You were supposed to tell me if you felt anything. Oh God, Sylvy."

"Ben, listen."

He gets an arm under my shoulder and tries to lift me off the chair. "Here, let's get you away from this thing."

I let him help me up but when he tries to lie me on the floor, I resist. "Wait. Listen to me. That won't work to stop this bug. You have to let me in with the infected people."

"What? No. No way. Sylvy, you might not even be infected, I can't let you expose yourself like that. It's crazy."

"It's the only way to save them."

Ben's shaking his head. "You're not making any sense. Just, let's lie you down and rest a minute."

"No. Ben. I know what I'm doing. You have to let me in there. I can help them."

"I... We don't even know if the door's open."

"Only one way to find out."

His lips become a thin line. "Okay, but if the door isn't open, there isn't anything we can do, and you're going to rest, deal?"

"Deal." Maybe. But maybe Liv could still get through some-how. Wait, what am I saying? Am I delirious? I'm going into a contagion zone on the word of a hallucination. But if it could save those people…

We're moving through the door and down the hall and I'm wearing a lab coat. Ben must've thrown it on me as we left the lab, but I don't remember doing so. My head's spinning and the world is coming in flashes: A hallway, a bloody handprint on the wall, a SWAT team member guarding a door, an exploded ceiling tile littering the floor with chunks of white crumble. Then we're here, at the glass room, and I can see them. I recog-nize three from the shelter from their driver's license photos and can guess which is Noi. Latrina is dead already. I know because her WHISP is gone, no longer shadowing her muscular arms and long braids, and there's a trickle of dry blood trailing from her pretty button nose. A man I don't recognize is also dead, but the rest are alive, more or less. Five are in the throes of seizures, bucking and shuddering in their restraints, while their WHISPs writhe in tandem. The last two are still and staring glassy eyed with blood oozing from their nostrils, so close to death, but yet, I can see their WHISPs.

"She needs to get inside."

I turn my head. Ben is addressing a set of three SWAT members in front of the door. One is connecting hoses to two large tanks. The other is focused on an exposed panel in the door's wide metal frame, a headlamp lighting up a mass of wires, circuitry, and C4.

The third must be supervising. "Actually, Doc, we're just about to attempt a temporary disarm to get in and get them out. You can treat them in the hallway."

No. No. NO. Too late! "I'm going in with you. I have to treat them now, right now. Look at them, they're dying."

The protest dies in his eyes when he sees my face, my

WHISP. "Fine, come in with us, but we'll only have," he looks at the man with the headlamp, "two minutes?"

The man doesn't look up as he take a hose line from the man with the tanks. "At most."

"Can I help?" Naomi is at Ben's side.

Ben nods. "I need you to get out of here. Take what data we have and get it to Lincoln in the house. I'll meet you there soon."

She nods, touches his arm. Turns to me. "I hope to get to know you better soon." Then she turns and runs away down the hall.

Temporary disarm. Two minutes, at most. Clarity like a knife to the heart rousts me from my stupor and sends blood into my cold hands and cheeks. "Ben. You have to go with her."

He faces me. "Not a chance."

My heart's pounding so hard I think it's going to burst through my ribs. "But—"

"It's time, folks. Whoever's coming in, we're going on my signal."

Even though I know it's no use, that Ben won't leave me, with the sting of salt in my eyes, I try one last time. "Please."

He kisses me and my heart melts into lava.

"Doc!"

I pull away. Frozen fog is pouring out of the hose held by the man with the headlamp onto the innards of the door panel, and the supervising SWAT member has his arm raised, while the one who was previously connecting hoses stands poised with his hands gripping the door handle.

"Now or never."

The supervisor drops his hand and the hose guy pulls the door open and everything stops. Tick. Tick. Tick. No boom. Hose guy rushes in and I'm right behind him wondering what the hell I'm going to do once I'm inside.

CHAPTER 28

Excerpt from Transcript of Session 52:
Dr. Aziz Fritz with Det. S. Harbinger

Harbinger: I forgot our anniversary.
Fritz: You have a lot going on, it's understandable.
Harbinger: It's not the first time either, but this time is the worst.
Fritz: How so?
Harbinger: Ben's been like Mr. Supportive Guy for years now.
Since before Lincoln developed a WHISP. Since the nightmare
about my parents started again. Really, he's a fucking saint, and
after twenty-four years of marriage, I can't even remember to buy
him a damn card.
Fritz: I'm sure he understands, but isn't there some way you
could make it up to him?
Harbinger: I'm always making things up to him.

I REACH THE NEAREST GLASSY-EYED MAN, PLACE A
hand on his forehead, turn my back so Liv is close to his
WHISP, and close my eyes. *Okay, Liv, do your stuff.* I visualize her
touching his WHISPs forehead, her hand sending out healing
signals to interrupt the WHISP bug. But it's too slow. There are

seven people in this room and I can't possibly get to them all in two minutes, especially not with SWAT trying to get them out. I raise my other hand toward the room at large, so Liv will do the same, and then I will energy through Liv's hand: calm energy, healing energy. It may all be in my head, but something, like thousands of shadowy, slippery, scuttling beetles, press back against us, trying to slip into the cracks between her particles.

No! My eyes fly open and two more, including Noi, have stopped moving and become glassy eyed and staring. It's not working. It has to work. I close my eyes again. *We can do this, Liv. We can do this.* I refocus and picture pure white light streaming from Liv's open hand, scattering the imaginary insects, frying them like an ant under a magnifying glass. The beams of light shoot out across the room and reach every living WHISPer. It lights their WHISPs from the inside, stills a buzzing in their particles. I can feel the vibrations strengthening, become more coherent and less chaotic. This will work. I just need to find the right frequency, like tuning a ham radio.

But then a new murky ooze creeps up into my chest. A different voice. An old voice. *You hate it. It would be so much easier without a WHISP. You'd never get that look of disgust again, never have to deal with people like the pizza boy again, and never have Ben look past you again.* I think of the victims from the shelter: hurt, unloved, rejected, hated, alone, for something they couldn't control. *You'll lose control and hurt someone just like Chester did. You're a monster now. A ticking time bomb. You know it's getting stronger every day. It's only a matter of time.* My resolve slips, the light fades, and onyx, skittering night returns. I sway on my feet, memories of the past year crashing down on me.

"One minute, Doc!"

No. This is ridiculous. Lincoln's had his WHISP for years and he's fine. I think of him and me sitting at a bench outside the lab having lunch together, laughing like we haven't laughed in years, laughing so much that soda gets up my nose and we laugh even harder. I think of Crone treating me exactly the same, and of the times another WHISPer looked at me and smiled. We're in this together. This isn't a cure and why should there be one? Because of psychopaths like Chester? They'll kill regardless, and would she even have been so violent against WHISPers if the world didn't hate them? Didn't hate her?

Yes, WHISPs still scare me. I'm not sure I'll ever get over that completely, but I don't want to live the rest of my life in constant fear of someone's shadow. Plus, Liv isn't just some thing, she's me, a part of me, anyway. Like, like…well, like nothing really, maybe my conscience, and Lincoln's WHISP is part of him. I can't keep being afraid of my own son, and I wouldn't cut off his arm just because it offended some people. No, fuck that. Fuck what some people think. Fuck what I used to think. We're a team now. Not even a team, just one person.

"Thirty seconds!"

Reaching out to Liv, I send the vibrating light again, willing her particles to calm the turmoil in the WHISP particles around us. The dark roiling mass recedes again. *That's it. Slow down. Find a calm steady balance. Stop the colliding impulses. Focus. Control.* I think it's working.

"Ten seconds! Doc, I've got to move him."

I open my eyes. The SWAT supervisor is there unstrapping the semiconscious man. The only live victims left are him and Noi, but the hose man is carrying out another woman. *Was I doing anything real?* I rush to Noi and attack a strap with fumbling fingers.

"Five seconds!"

The first strap is off. I move to the second. Out of the corner of my eye, Noi's WHISP shimmers. It's about to disperse. *Liv!* My hands go to Noi's forehead. I close my eyes. Millions of dark, angry bugs all chewing, burrowing, pulsating. They fill my brain. *Liv, help her!* I flood my mind with light: with the first time Lincoln grabbed my finger, the first time I kissed Ben, the day I made Detective. I see Lincoln graduating from high school, Ben and I exchanging wedding vows, the little kidnapped girl I found alive. Every wonderful memory I can muster. Calm, happy energy.

"Doc!"

"Sylvy!"

I open my eyes, tear through the final straps, and lift Noi under my arm. The door is just a few feet away. We're going to make it.

I trip and we both go down. Trying to cushion her dead weight, I land on my elbow on the concrete. Sickening pain rockets up my arm. Many-legged black things scrabble toward me. They're only a hallucination, right? My mind's illusion for the WHISP bug.

Am I delusional? Did I just infect myself? Is this all for nothing?

The last thing I see is Ben shoving his way through the door in a burst of light.

"SYLVY?"

I'm very cold. *Did I just die?*

"Sylvy, talk to me."

"What happened?" Opening my eyes, Ben's frowning face greets me. "Did it work?"

"Well, the door didn't blow up."

I shake my head as much as his cradling hands will allow. "The bug, the WHISPers." When I try to push myself up, jagged pain ratchets up my left arm.

"Easy. Easy. I think you broke your arm."

You think?

"I think you did it."

I grit my teeth. "Help me up."

He gently lifts me into a sitting position, and now I can see the hallway is filled with people. I don't think any are dead and none are seizing or in that glassy, comatose state. It's hard to tell though since they're lying on their backs on the floor as the SWAT members tend to them, bending over to check vitals. The supervisor sees me watching and gives a thumbs up. I assume that means everyone we got out is alive. Trying not to think of the two victims we were too late to save, or to look in the room at their corpses, I return the gesture with my good hand.

"We should call the ambulance back."

SWAT headlamp guy shakes his head. "I've been trying to get the house on the radio, but I can't. Must be too far underground here."

I look to Ben. "We should get up there, neither of us are doctors."

He shakes his head. "I'll go. How are you going to climb the ladder with a broken arm?"

Pushing against the wall with my good arm, I nod. "Good point. I—"

Two SWAT members come tearing down the hall toward us. I think one is Schmitty. The other, a woman, shouts when they get closer, "Filippo! Grania! Onodona! There's trouble at the house!"

"What?"

"That girl from the lab went over when we evac'ed and she said the other lab guy's gone and Chief Loman's been shot."

The three door SWAT members are up in an instant, the supervisor shouting, "Grania, you stay here with the survivors. Onodona, you're with me. Let's go." The four of them run back the way Schmitty and the woman came.

Ben face is taut with pain. "Lincoln."

It can't be. "Get me up."

Ben gets his arm under my good arm and hauls me to my

feet, but Grania turns to us. "Where do you think you're going?"

"My son was in that house," Ben's voice is hard as granite.

"Mine, too."

Grania blinks at us. Nods once. Then we're running down the hall following Schmitty and the rest, every step an explosion of pain in my arm. The hallway bounds around me like a bounce house, but I focus on Ben's back. When we reach the ladder, he turns to me, a question in his eyes.

"You go first. I'll hold onto your leg with my good arm."

A curt nod and he's climbing.

I grip his pant leg and hold on for dear life as I place first one foot on the rung and then the other. Trying to lean forward instead of back, we make our way slowly up. Each time my broken arm brushes the ladder, a bright flash blinds me with pain, but I hold on. Then Ben is out and lifting me by my good arm into the blustery cold.

"You okay?"

Nodding, I brush past him and sprint toward the house, my socks little protection against the cold, rocky ground. Some of the lights are on and I can see movement through the windows, but I can't tell if any of the outlines are Lincoln. Outpacing me in my socks, Ben passes me and sprints up the porch steps to the back door where he stops suddenly and puts his hands up.

"Don't shoot him! It's Ben!" Naomi comes out the back door and falls sobbing into Ben's arms.

I stop running. The cold air burns my lungs and my throat is raw meat, but nothing matters. It's true. From Naomi's reaction, I know in my heart it's true. Lincoln's gone. The frozen ground rushes up to meet me.

CHAPTER 29

Excerpt from Transcript of Session 39:
Dr. Aziz Fritz with Det. S. Harbinger

Fritz: Sylvia, how long have you been coming to see me now?
Harbinger: I don't know. About a year? Maybe a little longer.
Fritz: And knowing human nature through your work as a detec-
tive, is it your experience that people make sweeping changes in
their lives overnight, even under the best circumstances?
Harbinger: No. So what?
Fritz: So, I think it's time for you to accept that you are human
and therefore progress could take a long time. Cut yourself some
slack.
Harbinger: Are you sure you're not just drawing things out to
keep up your exorbitant hourly rates for another year?

BEEPS AND THE SMELL OF DISINFECTANT ANNOUNCE
I'm in the hospital again.

"Did we do it?"

I open my eyes. Ben is hunched over me, bloodshot, dark
circles, greasy hair, face drawn like a bad rendition of himself.

He touches my face. "Sylvy." He doesn't seem happy I'm

awake, doesn't crack a smile or try to make a joke about me and hospitals lately.

My blood turns to ice. "Ben, Jesus, what is it?" I try to push myself up, but find my arm immobilized in a sling. Then I remember the fall, the crack, but there's no cast. Not important. *Oh God.* I swallow hard. "Did they all die?"

He shakes his head. "No. I don't know what you did, but they all seem fine now, normal, consistent measurements."

"Even Noi?"

He nods.

"Then what's wrong? Am I still infected?"

He shakes his head and takes my good hand in his. "Sylvy, there's something I have to tell you." He takes a deep shuddering breath. "Lincoln..." His voice cracks.

"Oh my God. Did he get infected? What was he even doing there in the first place, Ben? Jesus!"

He squeezes my hand. "It's not that."

"Then what is it? You're scaring me." My head feels like it's full of cotton, and I know there's something I'm forgetting.

He swallows and wipes his eyes. "Remember when the Chief said that most of the SWATs had gone to get pizza?"

Pizza, what does that have to do with anything? "Yeah."

"Well, most of the others were in or around the barn and they didn't see what happened, but..." He chokes, swallows, and breathes again. "When Naomi got to the house, Lincoln was gone, all the paperwork he was working on was gone, and the Chief...the Chief's dead."

Gone. Dead. "What?" *No. No. What is he talking about?*

He nods. "Also, the van with the guards and scientists from the lab was assaulted on its way to the nearest state police post. All the state troopers in it are dead and the prisoners are gone, escaped."

What. The. Actual. Fuck. No, not important. Back up. "Lincoln's gone?" Memories thick as mud are coagulating in my mind. Running. Climbing the ladder with my injured arm.

"Forensics is going over the house inch by inch, but it looks like whoever was running that lab didn't want us to find out what they were doing and came back. When the barn was too guarded, they must've checked the house and found him there."

My baby boy. I can't breathe. "Was there blood?"

"Blood?"

"Lincoln's blood?"

Ben shakes his head. "I don't think so."

Okay, calm down. Still alive for now, probably. If they'd killed him, they would've left the body, like with Yosef. I look up at Ben. "We've got to find him, Ben."

He nods.

"I mean right now. Help me get out of this bed." Another kidnapping, another ticking clock, but this time, my son.

I expect a word of protest, but Ben just nods and starts unhooking wires.

SNEAK PEEK AT WHISPERS OF CONSPIRACY

WHISPS BOOK THREE

In every dream, a current of nightmare.
Lincoln is gone and it's all her fault. NYPD Detective Sylvia Harbinger once thought the world and its WHISPs had become the place of her nightmares, but now that her baby boy has been kidnapped by bioterrorists and taken halfway around the world, she knows what true nightmare is.

But Sylvia isn't about to abandon her son.

She'll do whatever it takes to get him back, even if it costs more than she ever thought possible to lose.

CHAPTER 1

Operation Shade: Debriefing SH – 00001 –
Audio Transcription Excerpt

*SH: Agent Casilla knows everything that I know about what
happened.*
Agent: I realize that. This is just a standard debriefing.
SH: Okay.
Agent: Why did you lie to the CIA?
*SH: I didn't lie. I failed to disclose information that wasn't asked
of me. There's a difference.*

Lincoln is gone. My baby is gone. And it's all my
fault.

"Sylvy?"

From the concern in Ben's eyes, he's said my name more
than once.

"Yeah."

"We're here."

I'd been staring out the window but seeing nothing. Now,
the entrance to the precinct looms over us. Before, the sight

would've filled my heart with a sense of home, but now, it's cold, foreign.

Ben clears his throat. "Do you want me to come with you?"

I shake my head. "No. They'll need you back at the lab. To go over anything…left behind." I open the car door, but he grabs my other hand.

"We'll *find* him."

I nod because I can't speak, not because I believe it.

He squeezes my hand before releasing it. I want to squeeze back, but my hand is numb, my body is numb. I can't feel the pavement beneath my feet as I get out and close the door behind me. A gust of wind catches my coat, throwing it open, but the bitter wind doesn't touch me. The cold comes from within, veins of ice pumping from my frozen heart, every breath a brittle pain in my chest.

I blink and I'm inside the building, crossing the first floor toward the stairs. Someone grabs my arm and spins me around.

"Harbinger!" Crone's face is an unhealthy shade of beetroot. "What are you doing here?"

I throw off his grip, my recently contused elbow screaming in protest. "My job." I turn back toward the stairs but he blocks me.

"No, not like this, you're not. Not right now. Look at yourself. You can barely stand."

"Get out of my way, Crone."

"No."

My fingers flit over the handle of my gun. "Get out of my way."

Crone doesn't budge. "I'm telling you this as your friend. You need to rest. You need to take some time."

"I need to find Lincoln."

"You will, but you won't do it today. Not like this."

"I'll do it any damn way I can and you're wasting time. This isn't your case. Get out of my way."

His eyes meet mine and he steps aside. "I just don't want you to ruin yourself."

I don't reply. His words echo like my footsteps in the stairwell. He doesn't have kids, he can't understand. Whatever happens to me doesn't matter. All I care about is Lincoln.

When I reach the basement, the Task Force floor is buzzing. People are everywhere. *Why wasn't there a response like this to the first kidnapping?* Then I see the state troopers mixed in among the crowd. The first kidnapping was one death and four missing. This is seven deaths and one kidnapping. This is bomb-wired rooms and computers erasing themselves, and evidence and people made to disappear.

"Harbinger?" Green stops in front of me.

"Where are we at?"

Her mouth works a moment before words come out. "Canvasing for witnesses to the Staties' van hit. Problem is, the van was in the middle of nowhere when it happened."

"Have we notified the airports, the border?"

She nods. "We've given them"—she swallows—"Lincoln's description and the best descriptions we have of the prisoners, the situation."

"What about the bodies? Where are we with IDs?"

"Running fingerprints, but no hits yet." Green pauses, winces.

"What?"

"You, um, you're shivering."

I wondered why it was hard to move my mouth properly. "I'll grab some coffee. Warm up." As if that were possible. "Forensics still sweeping the facility?"

She nods. "They aren't very optimistic. These people are too good."

No, no, no. I shake my head. "There has to be something. Nobody's that good."

"Harbinger?"

"Yeah."

"They could've killed him."

My blood turns instantly from ice to magma. "What?"

Green blanches. "I mean, Lincoln's still alive. There's hope."

The magma turns to stone. "I know."

"Okay. Good. Um, get your coffee and, um, there's a briefing in about an hour."

I nod then head to the break area, but when I bend to pick up a cup, my laptop bag strap slides down my arm and I realize I still have on my coat. I weave between bodies and make it to my desk to find it occupied by a Statie. I stand there for a minute, but he doesn't look up. I clear my throat.

"I'm kinda busy here." He's flipping through pages from a file.

"My desk."

He finally looks up. "Huh?"

"You're at my desk."

"Oh sorry, there wasn't anyone here." He makes no motions to leave.

My hands clench. Unclench. "I was in the hospital." His badge would just fit into his smug mouth, with a little assistance.

"Glad you're feeling better." He glances around. "There's not much room down here. Any chance we could share?"

Something shifts in the back of my mouth. A tooth. I pry open my jaw, the muscles of the joint creaking in protest. *Get the fuck out of my desk!* I set my laptop down on one side of the desk and take off my coat. I crumple it into a ball and drop it next to the desk. Turning away, I moderate my breathing as I work my way back to the coffee pot. He's working on the case, too, and chewing him out will do nothing productive. The scent of burnt coffee assaults my nose as I pour and my stomach lurches, bile splashing the back of my throat. In spite, I pull out milk from the mini-fridge and dump some into the cup, then add two sugars.

Back at my desk, I retrieve the wadded ball of my coat from the floor and pull a protein bar from the pocket. Ripping it open, I bite half off and chew methodically.

"I think some of the guys are ordering pizza later. You want in?"

I shake my head, the bar's claylike consistency making the mouthful impossible to swallow.

"Suit yourself, but I better not see you bogarting any slices of my meat-lovers."

Finally, the chewed mass goes down my throat. "You seem awfully chipper for just having lost seven of your compatriots." As soon as I speak, I wish I could choke down the words like the protein bar. They're cruel and stupid. A reflection of my own sourness, my own guilt, my own frustration.

The goofy smile melts away, his dark lips stretching thin, veiling his bright white teeth. "Hey, fuck you. I lost friends, good men who didn't deserve to get mowed down over some fucking"—at the last moment, his eyes find Liv and he stumbles in his rant—"research project."

Of course, I don't know exactly what he was about to say, but his face speaks volumes; he is no lover of WHISPs. A spark of anger flares then extinguishes. Who am I to judge? *I'm sorry.* I don't say the words. They'll sound hollow and be a waste of time, of breath. Instead, I shake my head. It doesn't matter. This doesn't matter. Only Lincoln matters. I open my laptop and bring it to life, ignoring my queasiness and the Statie's glare.

I'm not sure what I'm going to work on, what won't be repeating what others are already researching, but I need to do something, anything that feels like progress toward finding Lincoln. Maybe I can find construction permits or, at least, equipment rentals for the farmhouse. Someone had to build that laboratory underneath the barn. I wonder if I can request satellite photos of the area from Google or the NSA or somebody, maybe catch a license plate number or a face entering or leaving the lab. Or maybe I'm getting too fancy, and we should just check security cameras from the local gas stations. People working at the lab couldn't have just ghosted in and ghosted out. *Where to start?* My brain is spinning, but my fingers are idle on the laptop's keyboard. Maybe I should talk to Green first.

"Hey, Jerome!" A keen, thin Statie is suddenly at my side.

The Statie commandeering half my desk, Jerome, by his response, looks up. "Yeah, Mattie?"

"My source at that private airstrip came through." He thrusts a printed sheet at Jerome. "A private jet left the airfield last night headed for Turkmenistan. He said he didn't get a good look at who got on the plane, but said there were a bunch of trucks and that his boss got paid a stack of bills to keep the flight out of the records and to keep his mouth shut."

"Good work, Mattie, get—"

"Turkmenistan?"

Mattie barely spares me a glance. "It's a country in—"

"I know where it is." It's right smack dab in the middle of unethical WHISP research territory. I snatch the paper from Jerome's fingers. It looks like a flight plan.

"What the f—"

"They have my son."

I grab my coat off the floor and fish out my phone. The screen complains of a number of missed calls, but I dismiss them all and take a picture of the paper before handing it back to an open-mouthed Jerome. Standing, I address the other Statie. "Mattie is it?"

"Officer Matheson."

"Fine. Where is this airfield?"

Jerome stands and raises both hands palms out. "Whoa! What do you think you're doing? We'll report this at the briefing and State will figure out the best approach. This case may have started in the city, but it's in our jurisdiction now, and I'm not going to have you fuck it up. I'm sorry about your son, really, but I'm not even sure you should be working on this case anymore."

How dare you? Red spots blur my vision, but I take a deep, calming breath. Playing the grief-crazed mother won't earn me any points here. "First, I think you will find that the WHISP Task Force has statewide jurisdiction." *Truth.* "Second, with the Chief dead, I'm now in charge of the task force, so I can say who's on it and who isn't." *Possibly true.* I let out the rest of my breath because the truth of my next sentence crushes my heart. "And third, if that plane was carrying my son and really did leave the country, then this case is no longer under either of our jurisdictions anymore."

www.scarsdalepublishing.com

Also By Jen Haeger

Whispers of a Killer
WHISPS Book One